Robert S. Candlish

Reason and Revelation

SALZWASSER VERLAG

Robert S. Candlish

Reason and Revelation

Reprint of the original, first published in 1864.

1st Edition 2022 | ISBN: 978-3-75259-463-8

Verlag (Publisher): Salzwasser Verlag GmbH, Zeilweg 44, 60439 Frankfurt, Deutschland
Vertretungsberechtigt (Authorized to represent): E. Roepke, Zeilweg 44, 60439 Frankfurt, Deutschland
Druck (Print): Books on Demand GmbH, In de Tarpen 42, 22848 Norderstedt, Deutschland

REASON

AND

REVELATION.

By

ROBERT S. CANDLISH, D.D.

LONDON

1864.

CONTENTS.

Page

THE AUTHORITY AND INSPIRATION OF THE HOLY SCRIPTURES, ... 9

THE INFALLIBILITY OF HOLY SCRIPTURE, ... 53

CONSCIENCE AND THE BIBLE, ... 91

PAUL PREACHING AT ATHENS—REASON AND REVELATION, ... 131

THE DUTY OF FREE INQUIRY AND PRIVATE JUDGMENT, ... 161

Preface.

EDINBURGH, 15*th January* 1864.

I HAVE been, rather unexpectedly, asked by the Publishers to sanction a new issue of this little work, which, I thought, had gone very far into oblivion. So convinced was I of its being among forgotten things, that I had little scruple in using one of its treatises, revised and re-written, as my Introductory Lecture to the Students of the New College, at the opening of the present session. This has, somewhat to my surprise, led to my views on the subject of the Inspiration of the Bible being pretty freely canvassed. In point of fact, I have advanced no original views. All that I have said may be found, in germ and principle, in the works of Gaussen, Lee of Cambridge, and Tayler Lewis of America.* My object has been simply to place the doctrine which these writers, as well as others of older

* Dr. Lee's work is known to scholars. I hope we are soon to have a new edition of it, for it is invaluable. Tayler Lewis's little book has been republished in this country, with a recommendatory preface from the pen of one most competent to judge of its merits, the Rev. Dr. Henderson of Glasgow. I thoroughly agree with Dr. Henderson in all that he says in its praise. It is a singularly fresh, original, thoughtful treatise, and ought to be in the hands of all students and inquirers.

date, have scientifically expounded, in a plain and popular light. For it seems to me high time that this should be done. And the stir which my Introductory Lecture has occasioned makes me feel this more than ever. The real question must be fairly stated. My attempt to state it fairly—it is all that I have attempted—has been misunderstood in some quarters, and misrepresented in others. I mean to try to state it again in this preface.

I think I can best do this, in the way of offering some remarks on the references which have been made to my statements by Bishop Colenso and the Duke of Argyll. I do not class these two together, as of the same mind in this matter. Very far from it. I merely mean to say that I have now to deal, not with anonymous criticism, but with the comments of men high in Church and State.

The Prelate must take precedence of the Peer, being first in hand.

It is in the preface to the recently published fourth part of his "Pentateuch and Book of Joshua Critically Examined," that the Bishop does me the honour of mentioning me. And to what he says of me there I confine my attention.

His mode of quotation is peculiar.* Let the first of his three quotations serve as a specimen:—

---

* To prevent mistakes, I must explain that whatever I give of Colenso's book is given exactly as printed there; the italics, dashes, dots, &c., being all his own; ornaments of literature of his own devising. I have no fancy for them, and use none of them.

"*All that is in Scripture is not Revelation strictly so called*,—[which means, I suppose, 'All that is in the Bible, is not, in the strict and proper sense, the *Word of God*.'] To a large extent, Scripture is a record of human affairs—of the sayings and doings of men. *Is it to be held and considered infallible*, when it narrates the wars of kings, and inserts the genealogies of tribes and families, as well as when it announces an express oracle of heaven, or authoritatively promulgates Divine doctrines and commands?"—(Preface, pages xvii. xviii.)

Here I state a fact, and ask a question. My statement of the fact he breaks into two fragments—the first being significantly italicized—by an interpolated innuendo. The interpolation shows either gross ignorance or deliberate dishonesty. I impute to him only the former. He evidently does not know what "Revelation strictly so called" means. If he did, he could not have found such a world's wonder in so plain a truism as this,—that the Bible records not only what God says and does, but also what man says and does. I maintain strongly that "all that is in the Bible is in the strict and proper sense the Word of God." It is God's inspired and infallible record of his Revelation, and of the human affairs—the sayings and doings of men—with which it has pleased him that his Revelation should be mixed up. This is my answer to the question which I put,—as the Bishop must have known if he had read either my lecture or my book. He has the boldness to represent my putting of the question as implying the opposite answer. It is an artifice of controversy, happily not now common.

There is, indeed, in the Bishop's next quotation,* an

* "What God had to communicate to man, was to be communicated not all at once, but, as it were, piecemeal. This, I cannot but think, affords a strong pre-

attempt to convict me of inconsistency. It is a singularly constructed quotation, bringing together scraps from passages far apart, and dovetailing them ingeniously into a sort of mosaic pavement. To make one out, in that way, to be self-contradictory, may or may not be right and fair. But it can be neither right nor fair to say this of me,—not in the small type of a quotation, or quasi-quotation, from my book,—but in his own good, large-type, conclusive, summing up:—

"He still asserts his belief in an 'infallible guidance,'—an 'infallible superintendence,'—such as to maintain even a 'verbal accuracy.' But this does not extend to such matters as the 'wars of kings' and the 'genealogies of tribes and

---

sumption in favour of what is called plenary inspiration. It suggests a reason why God should from the very beginning, and all throughout, exercise such a superintendence over the committing of his communications to writing, as to secure even the *verbal accuracy* of the record..... Properly speaking, it (Holy Scripture) has but one author, the Holy Ghost, throughout. All the books of it are His; *He is responsible for them all:* and, being so, *He is entitled to the same measure of justice at our hands, which an ordinary writer may claim* (!).... It is not simply God speaking to man, and man listening to God. It is rather God coming down to earth, mixing Himself up with its ongoings, and *turning to His own account* (!) the sayings and doings of its inhabitants. Hence the need of discrimination..... I can see no reason why the HOLY SPIRIT (!) should not use the same latitude that a truthful man would use, when minute exactness is not necessary, and is not pretended,—as, for instance, in the use of round numbers, or in the customary ways of reckoning genealogies, or in the reporting of speeches, where the precise words are not material. Nay, more: I imagine that a man, writing under the assurance of Divine guidance, *might be even less careful than he would otherwise have felt himself bound to be* (!)..... I can well imagine that Evangelists and Apostles may have been led to use more freedom than they would otherwise have ventured upon in dealing with the Old Testament Scriptures, and connecting them with the New Dispensation, by the very fact of their being under *infallible guidance*..... I confess that, on any other supposition than that of *infallible guidance*, considering the usual scrupulosity of Jewish Doctors, with reference to the very letter of their sacred writings, the free mode of citation, practised by New Testament writers, seems to me all but inexplicable."—(Preface, page xviii.)

families,'—that is, I presume, to matters *non-essential* to human salvation,—in other words, to God's design in giving the Revelation."—(Page xix.)

It requires some stretch of charity to imagine that this is ignorant and not wilful misrepresentation. If he has read what he is quoting from, Colenso must know that I hold the exact reverse of what he here deliberately imputes to me. He is at liberty to argue,—which, however, he has not attempted to do,—that I cannot consistently hold the opinion which I avow. But he is not at liberty to assert that I hold the diametrically opposite opinion. This is what he has not scrupled to do.

Having made me say the contrary of what I do say, he goes on to refute the doctrine thus imputed to me:—

"The question then arises, as to what parts *are* essential, and what *not*. And of this, as Dr. Candlish does and must allow, *we* short-sighted creatures cannot possibly be the judges. *We* may imagine things to be essential, which in the plan and ordering of the Divine Wisdom are *not* essential; and therefore, though assuming an 'infallible superintendence,' we are utterly unable to judge *à priori* what parts of Scripture *must* be recorded with strict verbal accuracy."—(Page xix.)

Of course not. But that is the very argument which I have urged at some length for our belief that all "parts of Scripture must be recorded with strict verbal accuracy," if we are to be sure of our having what is "essential." Or, to put the statement in better Theology, if not in better English, I have argued that God, giving to us a Revelation of his mind and will, in the manner in which it has seemed good to him to give it,—that is, mixed up with mundane affairs and the sayings and doings of men,—secures its full and accurate conveyance to us,—and can secure that,—only by himself taking the oversight throughout of the very words in which the whole complex record is framed. This may be, in the Bishop's judgment, *à priori* assumption, to which he may prefer his *à posteriori* induction and investigation, (p. xix.) But at all events it is consistent with the doctrine of the plenary inspiration of all Scripture, which I hold. And it is inconsistent with the idea of our distinguishing, as to inspiration, between the essential and the non-essential in Scripture, which I repudiate and disown.

The Bishop's third quotation is also characteristic. He is very fond of arguing by means of brackets, italics, and notes of exclamation. It is an easy mode of arguing for him,—though somewhat irksome to his adversary. The mechanical costs less trouble than the mental. And it is convenient. It saves the giving of reasons; these figures of the press, if one may so say, being a cheap substitute for them.

He quotes a paragraph of mine,—making it fill half a page of his book,—with some half dozen interjections, a goodly array of sloped letters, and one very peculiar bracketed interpolation.* The interjections and sloped

* "There is need of continual discrimination, that we may ascertain the true value and bearing of scriptural statements, as expressive of the Divine Mind and Will. With ordinary candour, the task of exercising the necessary discrimination is not really difficult. But it is easy, if one is inclined, to create embarrassment,

letters may pass. Not so the interpolated parenthesis. It is this: "We human creatures, are 'in all fairness' to 'make allowance' for the Divine Being falling short of our standard of right, because He is subject to 'the constraining force of circumstances.'" My words, which he thus paraphrases,—having put them in italics of course,—are these: "In all fairness allowance ought to be made for the constraining force of circumstances." It is the end of a sentence, in which I say nothing whatever about "our standard of right," but speak only of "the highest ideal of pure truth and perfect holiness;"—and in which, moreover, I say not one word about "the Divine Being falling short of" anything, or "being subject to" anything, but speak only of what we must take into account in dealing with such a progressive development of his mind and will as he has given us in the Bible.

—to confound the earthly occasion with the heavenly lesson,—and to take exception to some things in the Divine procedure, which may appear to be inconsistent with the highest ideal of pure truth and perfect holiness, when *in all fairness allowance ought to be made for the constraining force of circumstances,* —[we human creatures, are 'in all fairness' to 'make allowance' for the Divine Being falling short of our standard of right, because He is subject to 'the constraining force of circumstances!'] We must regard God, in those dealings of His with men, which Scripture records, as *in some sense laid under a restraint* (!) It is no part of His purpose to coerce the human will, or to disturb and disarrange the ordinary laws, which regulate the incidents of human life, and the progress of human society. There *must* (!) be, on His part, *a certain process of accommodation.* He *cannot* (!) in His Word, any more than in His Providence, have things precisely such, and so put, as the standard of absolute perfection would require. In legislating, for instance, for ancient Israel, *it was not possible* to have the ordinance of marriage, the usages of war, the rights of captives, the relation of master and servant, and other similar matters affecting domestic order and the public weal, regulated exactly as absolutely strict principle demands (!)."

It is difficult to believe that an educated man like Colenso could so misrepresent me by mistake. But since he has misrepresented me, I must briefly explain my meaning.

I suppose that some things are impossible with God, from his very nature. "He cannot lie." "He cannot deny himself." These are scriptural statements. I suppose also that God, in dealing with his creatures,—especially his fallen creatures,—may resolve to lay himself under restraint,—or, in other words, may accommodate his procedure towards them to their state and circumstances. Perhaps, if he is to deal with them as still rational and free agents, he must do so. That, at all events, seems to have been our Lord's opinion, when he told the Jews of his day that Moses allowed their fathers a liberty of divorce, inconsistent with the original ideal of holy marriage at its first institution, "because of the hardness of their hearts" (Mark x. 2–9). I firmly believe that God was the author of the Mosaic law of marriage, as well as of the Adamic and the Christian. And I explain the admitted imperfection of the Mosaic law in this particular by the consideration, that God, having thought fit to assume the character of civil and political ruler and legislator over the Jews, did not scruple to adapt his law and policy, not always to his own perfect standard, but sometimes and in some respects to their state and circumstances; and that he must needs do so, if he was to rule them and legislate for them as rational and free agents. Is this limiting God? Is it at all derogatory to his absolute sovereignty and infinite perfection? Is it not rather a simple assertion of his unlimited power and discretion, as being at liberty to do always what, in the view of the case before him, he judges to be right?

It is precisely the same principle that I apply to the Bible, as the infallible record of an infallible Revelation. In determining the manner in which he is to reveal himself to men, and have his Revelation recorded, God must, of very necessity, lay down a plan, and in accordance with it, lay himself under conditions. And it is a perfectly fair and legitimate subject of inquiry,—what is that plan? and what are those conditions? Once, in giving the Law from Sinai, God spoke the words himself, and wrote them himself on tables of stone. Even then, he must needs adapt his Revelation to circumstances. He gave the Law otherwise than he would have given it to angels, or to man in Paradise. He gave it as "made for the lawless and disobedient" (1 Tim. i. 9). Nay more; when some forty years after he gave it again by the mouth of Moses (Deut. v.), he gave it, as it were, in a new edition, somewhat modified, at least in one of the commandments, to suit the condition in which the new generation of Israel was placed. May not this example show that God reveals his mind and will, not as realizing his own perfect ideal of optimism, but as in an important sense restrained from doing so? And, in truth, is he not necessarily thus restrained, if he is to deal with men and things as they are,—and so to deal with them as to effect his object in a way accommodated to them, as well as worthy of himself? What is this but saying that a father must communicate with his children, not according to his own powers and attainments, but according to their capacities and circumstances? Is it not simply what is said of our Lord: "With many such parables spake he the word unto them, as they were able to bear it"? (Mark iv. 33.)

What I have attempted is merely to apply this principle to the Bible as a whole. My method is plain enough. I assume or postulate, for the sake of argument, what seems to be the original plan, as existing in the mind of God, *à priori*, or beforehand. He means to communicate with men through men; and that, not once for all, but "at sundry times and in divers manners." I lay down certain conditions which, as it appears to me, must attach to the execution of such a plan. And I inquire how far these conditions may serve to explain the structure and aspect of the Bible as we actually have it; and, in particular, how far they go to account for certain facts or phenomena in the Bible that have been made objections to its infallibility as the plenarily, or verbally, inspired word of God. I may have fallen into error, in forming my notion of the plan, or in laying down the conditions, or in applying them to the facts or phenomena in question. But I still think that my method is a safe and right one. And, at all events, I hold myself entitled to assert that it is consistent with my believing that every word of the Hebrew and Greek Scriptures—in so far of course as the right reading of texts can be critically ascertained—is divine as well as human; that every word of the Bible is what it is, and where it is, by the direct will of the Holy Spirit, as truly as by the purpose of the writer; that the Holy Spirit is responsible for its being what it is and where it is; that it is the Holy Spirit's word as much as the writer's. Only the Holy Spirit does not supersede the writer, or make him write unnaturally. That is really all.

I have read with admiration the Duke of Argyll's speech at Glasgow (11th January 1864); and for many things in it I thank him most cordially. I appreciate also the honour he has done me in alluding to this work which I am now republishing; and I am very sure that he had no intention of doing anything else than full justice to the views which I hold. I do not know how far my views may quite agree with his. But I think it needful to offer a word or two of explanation as to the two very brief sentences which His Grace quotes, and as to the connection in which he quotes them.

Referring to the difficulty sometimes felt in receiving

certain doctrines of astronomy and geology, on the ground of their apparently conflicting with Scriptural statements, and to certain old ways of dealing with it,—the Duke asks, "How do we get over that difficulty now?" And he answers as follows:—

"I believe we get over that difficulty simply by adopting a doctrine which is not authoritative, which is not traditional, which is objected to by the Holy Catholic Church, as the Bishop of Oxford calls it, for many generations—I mean this, which I find very ably expressed by Dr. Candlish in a work recently published, called 'Reason and Revelation,' as follows:—'All that is in Scripture is not necessarily revelation; to a large extent the Bible is a record of human affairs—the sayings and doings of men, not a record of divine doctrine or of communications from God.' And, especially in reference to physical facts, Dr. Candlish asserts, as I believe he well may, the independence of our faculties, in this important passage: 'The inspired word is abreast of the science and literature of its own age, but not in advance of it.' That is how we get out of the difficulties—not by holding to traditional and authoritative interpretations belonging to the Holy Catholic Church, but by maintaining the independence of our own judgments on all questions on which our own judgments are competent investigators of truth, and submitting to the conclusion which is manifest, that physical truth is only brought into connection with the Bible as a means of illustration. And now, when we come to look at it in this point of view, when we recollect that the Bible reveals, not physical, but spiritual truth, we shall find that not one of the discoveries of modern science touches in the slightest degree the revelation which is made to us."—(*Report in "Morning Journal," Jan. 12.*)

Perhaps I have already dealt sufficiently with the first of these quotations from my book. The Duke introduces it merely as preliminary to the second: "The inspired word is abreast of the science and literature of its own age, but not in advance of it."

That is what I say, no doubt; but it is not all that I say. And it is scarcely fair to represent it as all that I say; for, in fact, I say the very opposite of the view which may be held to be here ascribed to me.

I affirm that the inspired word is so framed as to be

found consistent with the science and literature of ages long posterior to its own. This is the very point and pith of my argument. I put it as a problem which only the Omniscient can solve,—How a Revelation which is to range over centuries of comparative ignorance on matters of secular and mundane science,—and is necessarily, according to its plan, to mix up these matters freely with its higher themes,—is to be so constructed, and so recorded, that it shall not anticipate human discoveries, and yet shall be in entire harmony with them as in the course of time they emerge. I maintain that this precise problem is found actually solved, in point of fact, in the Bible. And I draw the inference that this implies its plenary, verbal inspiration. The reason is plain enough, according to my view. Only One seeing the end from the beginning could so adjust the language used as, on the one hand, to make it tell the men of the existing generation no more than they otherwise knew of astronomical, or geological, or other natural truth;—and yet, on the other hand, to make it such that the men of all future generations should be able in the long run, and without violence, to explain it satisfactorily, in the light of their clearer and fuller information, and their more advanced and accurate science.*

* See page 85, where I refer to a very interesting remark of Hugh Miller's as to the difference in this respect between the uninspired Westminster Standards and the inspired books of Moses, with reference to the language which they respectively use i speaking of the creation of the world.

I am not quite sure that I quite understand the Duke of Argyll's statements upon this point. So far as I can gather, I scarcely think that they altogether coincide with mine; or that there is such an agreement as His Grace seems to suppose. I may be doing him injustice; but I rather imagine that he is prepared to admit, not only apparent, but real, discrepancies between the statements of the Bible and the facts of science.* Of course that admission requires some modification of the doctrine of plenary or verbal inspiration. In my opinion the admission is unnecessary. All past experience, I think, goes to prove it to be unnecessary. Always hitherto it has been found that, after a little time, and a little patience on both sides, apparent discrepancies have turned out not to be real. I am prepared to expect that the same final harmony will come out of passing discord, in the future progress of Biblical study and scientific research,—independently conducted

* I am almost forced to infer this from the closing words of the passage: "When we recollect that the Bible reveals, not physical, but spiritual truth, we shall find that not one of the discoveries of modern science touches in the slightest degree the revelation which is made to us." Of course I hold, with the Duke, that "the Bible reveals, not physical, but spiritual truth." That, no doubt, is its proper, primary design. But then I hold that it reveals spiritual truth in connection with physical truth; and that, on the plan which God has seen fit to adopt, it could not have revealed spiritual truth otherwise. And I hold that it could not, on that plan, reveal spiritual truth infallibly, unless it were infallible also in all that it says about physical truth. In other words, all its references to physical truth must be true; God being, if without offence I may so say, responsible for them. They are references merely *de presenti*, and not discoveries *de futuro*;—far less are they absolute declarations of the highest order ultimately to be developed in the universe. Still they are so framed that, while they anticipate nothing, they are in harmony with all that is ever to be known.

and with Baconian modesty on both sides,—without rash or premature dogmatism or generalization on either. In that confident expectation, I can calmly await the issue.

I close with one remark. It is the policy of our opponents, on this question, to run us up to untenable positions. They insist on our maintaining certain extreme and absurd views, such as have no doubt sometimes found supporters among theologians writing before the subject was much discussed. And they raise a shout of exultation when any rational explanation is given on our side, as if it implied an entire abandonment of the whole doctrine. We have to thank Coleridge and Arnold for having led the van in this unworthy mode of assault. They, however, I believe, did it ignorantly; not knowing, or not understanding, the real orthodox belief, as expounded by its intelligent advocates. I am not prepared to be quite so charitable in my judgment of some, at least, of the tribe who have so eagerly caught up the weapon wielded by these great men. It is far easier to ring the changes on the word "mechanical,"—and to raise a rude laugh at the idea of the inspired writers being made mere receptacles or "drawers,"—and so forth,—than to enter seriously into the discussion of what all earnest persons must allow to be a difficult and delicate, as well as a very sacred, topic of investigation.

For our part, we must beware of being too much moved by the taunts of such adversaries. And, in particular, we must beware of permitting them to drive us into asserting more than Scripture itself and sound reason fairly warrant and require. It is on this account that I am not myself very sensitive on the score of being charged by hostile critics with surrendering the high views of Inspiration commonly held in the Evangelical Churches, because I endeavour to make some small contribution towards a fair and candid exposition of what these views, when candidly looked at, really are. And on the same ground, I consider that a fair appeal may be made to some friendly parties to whom some things I have been advancing may have occasioned uneasiness. They need not prematurely take alarm, as if the foundations of the citadel of God's inspired word were to be destroyed, or even weakened. Perhaps they may not hitherto have been led to walk about these foundations very closely. Perhaps, also, they may not be accustomed to draw the distinctions which it is needful to draw when a complex object, such as either the written word, or the Incarnate Word,—uniting the human and the divine,—is under examination. I would suggest the propriety of their putting the best construction they can on attempts made to clear up what has been too often, whether unintentionally or on purpose, involved in mist and doubt. And for myself, I claim the justice of being believed when I avow it as my sole aim to advocate, as best I may, the great truth on which the religion of Christ and the hopes of Christians depend,—that not only is the word of God in the Bible, but that the Bible is itself, in the strictest and fullest sense, in every particular of its contents and in every expression which it uses, the infallible word of the one only living and true God.

THE AUTHORITY AND INSPIRATION

OF

THE HOLY SCRIPTURES.

THE AUTHORITY AND INSPIRATION

OF

THE HOLY SCRIPTURES.

THE authority and inspiration of Holy Scripture form one subject. According to its inspiration, so is its authority. And if the Bible is not inspired, in the full sense of that term,—in the sense of its being literally the word of God,—the whole question as to the degree of weight to be attached to its statements becomes a matter of discretion and doubt. Reason, or intuition, or whatever else the knowing faculty in man may be called, is constituted the ultimate and only judge. And in all that relates to our acquaintance and intercourse with the Supreme,—in the whole vast problem of the settlement of our peace with God, and the adjustment of the terms on which we are to be with him for ever,—we have absolutely no distinct and authoritative expression of the Divine mind at all. We are left entirely to the guidance of the higher instincts of our own nature, and of such finer particles of the historical Record,—such flowers of Biblical fact or argument or appeal,—as these instincts may happen to grasp. In short, we have no external standard or test of religious truth,—no valid objective revelation,—no "thus saith the Lord;"—but only such a measure of insight as a good and holy man, by the help of what other good and holy men have written, may attain into the Divine Ideal, which the aching void and craving want of the human soul either creates and evokes for itself, or welcomes when presented from whatever quarter, and by whatever means.

This is especially the state of the question with reference to the turn which modern speculation, in religious matters, has taken.

For a revolution, as it would seem, has come over the camp and kingdom of the freethinkers—whether philosophers or divines.

Formerly, the battle of the Bible was to be fought chiefly on the ground of historical testimony and documentary evidence. The possibility at least,—if not the desirableness,—not to say the necessity,—both of an express revelation from above, and of an infallible record of that revelation,—was acknowledged;—and upon that acknowledgment the method of procedure was well defined. Two steps were required. In the first place, good cause must be shown for connecting the two volumes which we now call the Old and New Testaments, and these alone, with the entire body of proof for the supernatural origin of our religion, which miracles, prophecy, internal marks of credibility, and other branches of the evidence of a divine revelation, afford. And in the second place, these volumes being thus attested and accredited—by the whole weight of proof that accredits and attests the religion itself with which they are identified,—it followed that they must be allowed to speak for themselves, as to the manner in which they were composed, and the measure of deference to which they were entitled. Thus the two questions, of the canon of Scripture, and the authority of Scripture, fell to be discussed in their order, immediately after the evidences of Revealed Religion. The divine origin of Christianity being established by the usual arguments, together with the genuineness and authenticity, as historical documents, of the books from which we derive our information concerning it—the way was open for inquiring, *first*—On what principle have these books come to be separated from all other contemporary writings, so as to form one entire and select volume—the Holy Bible—held to possess a peculiar character, as entitled to be considered exclusively and *par excellence* divine? And, *secondly*,—In what sense, and to what extent, is the volume thus formed to be regarded as the word of God,—how far is it to be received as dictated by his Spirit, and as declaring to us authoritatively his mind and will? This last inquiry, supposing the other to have been satisfactorily adjusted, sought and found its solution within the volume itself; and whatever it could be fairly proved that the Bible claimed to be, in respect of its inspiration,—that, it was admitted, it must be allowed and believed to be. For at that stage of the Christian argument, the Bible had established a right to speak for itself, and to say what kind and amount of submission it demanded at the hands of all Christian men.

Such is the method of proof applicable to this subject, as it used to be discussed formerly, in the Protestant schools and books of divinity. And such, I venture to think, is the only fair and legitimate method of proof still; at least, if the sound and cautious principles of the Baconian logic, or the inductive philosophy, are to have any weight in the province of religious belief. By a rigid investigation of its credentials, we ascertain that Christianity is the true religion,—that it is of supernatural origin,—that it is a divine revelation, divinely attested. On an examination of written records and documents, we find, that this religion of Christianity, thus proved to be divine, is identified with a volume entirely *sui generis;*—that the whole force of its own divine authority, and of the divine attestations on which it leans, is transferred to that volume;—that the volume, in short, is the religion which has been proved to be divine, and is therefore itself divine. Thereafter, we consult the volume itself to discover what it tells us of its own composition and claims: and whatever it tells us concerning itself, we now implicitly receive as true.

But a new aspect of the question meets us, as we come in contact with the speculations of modern times. Not only the antecedent probability, but the very possibility of an infallible external standard of faith, is doubted at least in some quarters, and wholly denied in others. A subtle sort of refined mysticism,—offspring of the transcendental philosophy meeting with a certain vague fervour of evangelical spirituality,—has entered the field: and the atmosphere has become dim with the haze and mist of a vapoury and verbose cloud, in which nothing is clear, nothing distinct or defined, but the vast sublime of chaos seems again to brood over all things.

Among others who have contributed to this result, Schleiermacher in Germany might be named, and the poet Coleridge among ourselves; although it is due to our great and good countryman to remark, that many who are indebted to him,—and these not merely among the more openly sceptical, but even among the schools and circles of far more evangelical thinkers,—have improved upon his hints, bettered his example, and so out-Coleridged Coleridge that the philosophic bard might with almost as much justice protest against being identified with his followers, as Wilkes the patriot did when he denied that he had ever been a Wilkite.

At the same time the impulse given by the profound and transcendent genius of Coleridge, has been one chief cause or occasion of the style and method that has become fashionable, of late years, in treating of the inspired authority of the Bible. His famous opprobrium of Bibliolatry,—flung in the face of old-school, Bible-loving, gospel-taught Christians,—has become a by-word and watchword in the mouths of men, whom to name in the same breath with Coleridge would be to offend alike against high intellect and pure spirituality. Even some minds of better mark, while themselves railing against the mere echoes with which, instead of voices, they say the orthodox world resounds, have not scrupled to ring the changes on this poorest of all echoes,—the unintelligent echo of a not very intelligible conceit,—filling the air with the cry of Bible-worship, and making it out that to receive the Bible as the word of God is as gross idolatry and superstition as to revere the Pope in the character of the Vicar of Christ.

With this modern form of opposition to the infallibility of Holy Scripture, it is not very easy to deal. In the first place, it is in itself very intangible, unfixed, obscure; being negative rather than positive. And it is apt, moreover, to take shelter in a sort of studied indistinctness; making a merit of abstaining from plainness of speech, and creating such a vague alarm as leads timid men to be thankful for any measure of forbearance, and to shrink from asking explanations, or wishing to have the inquiry carried further home.

A notable instance of this occurs in a tract of Archdeacon Hare, in which he speaks of himself and those who think with him, as "finding difficulty in the formation and exposition of their opinions on this mysterious and delicate subject,"—"hesitating to bring forward what they felt to be immature and imperfect," and "shrinking from the shock it would be to many pious persons if they were led to doubt the correctness of their notions concerning the plenary inspiration of every word of the Bible."[1] So far good. This may be a reason why "refusing to adopt the popular view on the subject, the Archdeacon does not straightway promulgate another view." But might not this hesitancy of his incline him to speak a little less offensively of the popular view than he sometimes does, seeing that he has nothing better to

[1] Letter to the Editor of the English Review, p. 26.

put in its place?[1] Might it not also suggest the suspicion that possibly he does not really understand that "popular view" itself so well as he evidently thinks he does? And, above all, does it never occur to him that this sort of bush-fighting is unfair to his opponents, and that they are entitled to demand from him a practical repudiation of the popish doctrine of reserve—as well as a distinct, articulate, and manly avowal of what he, and such as he, really hold the Scriptures of the Old and New Testaments to be?

But I must do what I can to thread my way through the misty labyrinth. And accordingly, passing from preliminaries, I now propose to indicate rather than discuss—for I can do little more than indicate—four successive topics, as those which, in my opinion, a thorough inquiry into the subject before us should embrace.

I. The conditions of the question should be ascertained. What previous points of controversy are to be held as settled? And what meaning is to be attached to the terms employed?—II. The method of proof ought to be

---

[1] The Archdeacon in his "Mission of the Comforter" (Appendix, p. 500), quotes from Akermann, with a manifest adoption of the sentiment as his own, a passage in which that author speaks of the position of the writers of the Bible, on the theory of plenary inspiration, as being the position of "drawers wherein the Holy Ghost puts such and such things,"—whose "recipiency, with reference to the Spirit inspiring them, was like that of a letter-box." Is any man entitled thus to caricature, distort, and insult the opinion deeply and devoutly held by his fellow-Christians and fellow-countrymen, and yet to make a merit of his refusal to state explicitly and unequivocally his own views, which he would substitute in its stead? If he says he has no views that he can explicitly and unequivocally state, that is another matter. Let him say so; and let the controversy be adjusted accordingly. But let him not affect the praise of tenderness to tender consciences and scrupulous understandings, without explaining what he means.

adjusted. What are the lines of evidence bearing upon the investigation? And what is their precise amount and value, whether separately or in combination?—III. The sources of difficulty are to be candidly and cautiously weighed. And IV. The practical value of the doctrine is to be estimated, with especial reference to the right fixing of the limits between divine authority and human liberty, and the vindication of our Protestant submission to the teaching of the Spirit, in and by the word, from the imputation of its being analogous to, if not virtually identical with, the popish prostration of the intellect, and heart, and will, beneath the blind sway of a spiritual monarch or a traditional Church. These, then, are my heads of discourse.

I. There are several preliminary matters in regard to which we ought to have a clear and common understanding, before we enter directly upon the argument we have in hand. Three of these in particular must be briefly noticed, however imperfectly.

1. A divine revelation of the mind of God is a different thing from a divine action on the mind of man. To some, this remark may sound like a self-evident truism; but the turn of modern metaphysical speculation in certain quarters renders it necessary to make it.

According to what is now a favourite theory of our mental constitution, we are possessed of a twofold reason; the one, the lower, or logical faculty, which deals with truth in the region of experimental knowledge, and deals with it mediately, through the processes and forms of ratiocination and language; the other, the higher, or intuitional faculty, which has for its object the spiritual, the transcendental, the infinite, and which grasps its object immediately, by a sort of super-sensual instinct, and without the intervention of the ordinary means, or *media*, of human thought. To the cognisance of this latter faculty belongs the idea of God, and of whatever pertains to his character, government, and law. Whatever real insight we have into the being and perfections of God, is by the intuitional faculty, or by intuition. Hence it is inferred that the only way in which God can make discoveries of himself to man, is by quickening his intuitional faculty, and so giving to his higher reason a new sense and sight of things divine. In this way all revelation is resolved into one grand process of subjective illumination, which God has been carrying on by a great variety of methods since the world began. In short, according to the theory to which I am now adverting, revelation is not oracular, but providential. The Scriptures are not in any proper sense the oracles of God;—nor do they convey to us direct utterances, or objective communications, of the divine mind. They merely contain materials fitted to exercise a wholesome influence, by awakening into more intense and lively action our own intuitional powers, through the contagion of sympathy—the force of example—and whatever divine impulse may lead us to kindle our torch at the divine fire which we see burning there so brightly.

For that a divine fire does burn in the Bible is not denied. It burns in the wondrous history of the Church as unfolded in the Bible, from the first germ of that history in the homes of the pilgrim patriarchs—through all the stirring vicissitudes in the Jewish annals of captivity, deliverance, wilderness-wanderings, wars, and victories, gorgeous pomps, and temple services—down to the full development of faith and fellowship ushered in at Pentecost. It burns also in the heroic lives and deaths —the words and deeds—of all the holy men of whom the world was not worthy—the martyrs, prophets, apostles, raised up in succession to receive the gift of a divine intuition, and spread the savour of a divine unction all around. Especially it burns in the character and life of the divine Man who taught in Galilee and Judea, and died on Calvary.

Thus, throughout the Bible a divine fire burns. The sympathising student may catch the flame of it; and in this way, imbibing the spirit of the Scriptural narratives, —and of the Scriptural personages whom these narratives, so manifestly show to have been spiritually moved,—being moreover spiritually moved himself,—he may gain an insight into things divine, otherwise beyond his reach. Thus in a sense he may come to "see Him who is invisible."

Now this vague and perhaps sublime recognition of a certain sort of divinity in the Bible, is manifestly inconsistent with the idea of its being, in any fair meaning of the term, a revelation of the mind of God. It becomes, in this view, merely one of the means by which God acts upon the mind of man. The Bible is in no respect different from "Fox's Book of Martyrs," or "The Scottish

Worthies," in which also the divine life is manifested through the actions and sufferings of divinely-gifted and divinely-aided men. There may be a difference in degree between God's teaching us thus in the Bible, and his teaching us in the same way in these other works. But there is no difference in kind.

To call this a revelation is an abuse of language; but it is a plausible abuse, and one fitted to impose upon the unwary. The distinction between a real revelation and this spurious counterfeit adroitly substituted for it, is as broad as it is vital. It may be made clear by a simple illustration.

It is one thing for a king to leave his subjects to gather his mind from what they may see of the conduct of his officers and captains, whom he admits nearest to his person, and who may be presumed to have the best opportunities of knowing him, and to be most strongly attached to him by the ties of loyalty and love;—to be most capable, therefore, of exhibiting and acting out, in their whole life and conversation, the true spirit of their royal master's kingdom. It is quite another thing for the king to make an express communication of his mind to his subjects, and to use the agency of his officers and captains in making it. That nothing is to be learned of his mind in the first of these two ways I am far from saying; nay, I admit that the teaching of the Bible is, in many parts, of that indirect nature, in so far at least as the use which we are to make of its inspired narrative is concerned. Still revelation, properly so called, is something different. It is not merely a depository or receptacle of sundry influences fitted to act upon my mind. It is God himself making known to me, and to all men, his own mind. It is God speaking to man.

2. Inspiration, as connected with revelation, has respect, not to the receiving of divinely communicated truth, but to the communication of it to others. This again might seem so self-evident as scarcely to need its being stated. But in certain quarters there is great confusion of ideas upon this very point.

It is admited by all deep thinkers—it is a great doctrine of Scripture, that spiritual things can only be spiritually discerned. Let these spiritual things be set forth ever so clearly, in the plainest forms of speech, so that an intelligent man can have no difficulty in ascertaining what is meant, and in laying down correct propositions upon the subjects to which they relate, still the things themselves cannot be fully grasped by the mere logical faculty or understanding; the higher reason or intuition, which alone is conversant with the infinite and the absolute, must be called into exercise; and even it cannot take in the things of the Spirit of God, to the effect of their becoming practically and powerfully influential, without an operation of that same Spirit upon the mind itself, purging, quickening, elevating the mental eye, so as to make it capable of the divine, the beatific vision.

All this is true; or, in other words, it is true that no communication of the mind of God to me from without, even if it were made to me directly and immediately, in express terms, by God himself, could give me a real spiritual, satisfying, and saving knowledge of God, if he did not also, by his Holy Spirit, touch and move me within in my inner man, giving me a spiritual tact and spiritual taste to discern spiritual things.

Now, such an action of the Spirit of God in and upon my spirit, with a view to my spiritually apprehending spiritual truth, may be called in a certain sense inspiration. And if there be due warning given of the unusual sense in which the word is to be employed, no great harm perhaps may be done.

But such an application of the term ceases to be harmless, and becomes a snare or a juggle, when it is the occasion of confounding the Spirit's action upon me, for my own enlightenment and edification, with the use which the Spirit may make of me, for conveying his mind to others. The inspiration of a disciple is one thing; the inspiration of an apostle is another.

A little child in the kingdom of God is inspired: he is breathed upon,—he is breathed into,—by the Holy Spirit; he has imparted to him a capacity for knowing God and apprehending things divine, higher far than man's proudest intellect can boast. He has a God-given eye to see, and a God-given heart to feel, the very eye and heart of the Eternal Father, as he looks down from heaven in love, to embrace all that believe in his Son. Tender as he may be in age, and but ill-instructed in the schools of human learning, that little child has in him the Spirit who "searcheth all things, even the deep things of God;" and in respect of all that pertains to his saving acquaintance with the Most High, he may be greater than the greatest of the prophets.

Nevertheless there is an inspiration proper to the

prophet, as a revealer of the will of God, which the little child, as a learner of it, does not need, and does not possess. This last sort of inspiration may be less intuitional and spiritual, so far as the immediate recipient of it is concerned, than the other; and therefore to him personally, far less valuable. It would have been better for Balaam personally, if he had been taught as a little child by the Spirit to know the will of God, for his own salvation, rather than used as a prophet by the Spirit, almost as involuntarily as his own dumb beast, for making known the will of God to others. The question here, however, is not as to the comparative advantages of these two operations of the Spirit, but as to the essential distinction between them. Our sole concern at present is not with what the Spirit does when he works faith in the heart, but with what he does when he employs human instrumentality for communicating those truths which are the objects of faith.

3. One other remark, under this head, must be allowed. The fact of inspiration is a different thing altogether from the manner of it. The fact of inspiration may be proved by divine testimony, and accepted as an ascertained article of belief, while the manner of it may be neither revealed from heaven nor within the range of discovery or conjecture upon earth.

But it may be asked, What are we to understand by the fact of inspiration which is to be proved? And especially, What are we to understand by the inspiration of the Bible?

To this I answer generally, that I hold it to be an

infallible divine guidance exercised over those who are commissioned to declare the mind of God, so as to secure that in declaring it they do not err. What they say or write under this guidance, is as truly said and written by God, through them, as if their instrumentality were not used at all. God is in the fullest sense responsible for every word of it.

Now I do not much care about the definition of the term being more precise than this. It is of very little consequence whether you call this verbal dictation or not. It is equivalent to verbal dictation, as regards the reliance which we may place on the discourse, or the document, that is the result of it. Only to speak of it under that name is to raise a question as to the manner of inspiration, the very subject into which I refuse to be dragged. For the same reason, I refuse to discuss a topic which used to be too much a favourite among religious writers, that of the different kinds and degrees of inspiration necessary for different sorts of composition. The mode of divine action upon the mind of the speaker, or writer, is not the point at issue. It is enough to maintain such an action as makes the word spoken, and the word written, truly and all throughout, the very word of God.

Oh! but this is a mechanical theory of inspiration, cry some. We, for our part, prefer the dynamical. The prophets and apostles were dynamically inspired, not mechanically.

Formidable words! which it would puzzle many who use them most familiarly to translate into plain English, and plainly distinguish from one another.

But if what they mean is this; that God by his

Spirit cannot so superintend and guide a man speaking or writing on his behalf, as to secure that every word of what the man speaks or writes shall be precisely what God would have it to be; and that not merely the whole treatise, but every sentence and syllable of it, shall be as much to be ascribed to God as its author as if he had himself written it with his own hand; if they mean that God cannot do this, without turning the man into a mere machine—if this be what they mean—then I have to tell them that the *onus probandi*, the burden of proof, lies with them. They must give some reason for the limitation which they would impose upon the divine omnipotence. They must show cause why God may not employ all or any of his creatures infallibly to do his will and declare his pleasure, according to their several natures, and in entire consistency with the natural exercise of all their faculties.

God may speak and write articulately in human language without the intervention of any created being, as he did on Sinai. He may cause articulate human speech to issue from the lips of a brazen trumpet, or a dumb ass. He may constrain a reluctant prophet to utter the words he puts in his mouth, almost against his will, as in the case of Balaam: or so order the spontaneous utterance of a persecuting high priest, as to make it an unconscious prediction, as in the case of Caiaphas. But is he restricted to these ways of employing intelligent agents infallibly to declare his mind and will?

Let us see how this matter really stands. Let us eliminate and adjust the conditions of the problem.

It is an important part of the divine purpose that, for the most part, men should be employed in declaring his mind and will to their fellow-men; men rather than, for example, angels. Several good reasons may be assigned for this. Two, in particular, may be named here.

For the purposes of evidence, this is an important arrangement. A divine revelation needs not only to be communicated, but to be authenticated; and the authentication of it must largely depend upon human testimony. Take, for example, the four gospels. These are not merely the records of our Lord's ministry, but the proofs of it. It is upon the historical authority of these documents that we believe Christ to have been a historical personage, and to have said, and done, and suffered the things ascribed to him. But the historical authority of the gospels rests very much, not only on the external evidence in their behalf afforded by the writers of the first and second centuries, but also on the internal evidence arising out of a comparison of them among themselves. And here great stress is justly laid upon their essential agreement, amid minute and incidental differences. There are variations enough in the accounts which they severally give of Christ, to preclude the idea of a concerted plan, or of premeditated collusion; while there is so entire a harmony throughout as to make it manifest that they are all speaking of a real person, and that person the same in all. In short, we have four independent witnesses to the facts of our Lord's history; proved to be independent, by the very differences that are found in their depositions; differences not sufficient to invalidate the testimony of any of them, but only fitted to enhance the value of the whole, by making it clear that they did not conspire together to deceive.

Such is the actual result of a fair collation and comparison of the four gospels as they stand.

Now to secure that result, it is manifest that the Spirit, in inspiring each evangelist, must act according to that evangelist's own turn of thought and gift of memory, and must direct him to the use of expressions such as shall at once convey the mind of the Spirit in a way for which he can make himself thoroughly responsible, and shall also at the same time record the *bona fide* deposition of the evangelist, as a witness to the transactions which he narrates.

Nor is there any incompatibility between these two things. Take an illustration. Let it be supposed that any one—say such an one as Socrates—has spent three years in teaching, and that he wishes an authentic and self-authenticating record of his ministry to go down to posterity. Four of his favourite pupils; or two, perhaps, of these, and two other students writing upon the immediate and personal information of men who had been pupils, prepare four separate and independent narratives, all availing themselves more or less of the reminiscences current in the school. The four narratives are submitted to the revision of Socrates. He is to correct and verify them, so as to make each of them a record for which he can become himself out and out responsible. And yet he is not to prune and pare them into an artificial sameness. Would he have any difficulty in the task? Could he not easily revise each narrative, with such close attention to the minutest turn of phraseology as to imply that he sets his seal to every word of it, and owns it to be what he is prepared to stand to as an exact record of his sayings and doings? And would he ever dream of reducing all the four to one flat level of literal uniformity? Would he obliterate all the nice and delicate traces of truth and character that are to be observed in different varieties of men, honestly and correctly testifying, each according to his own genius, to the same fact, or to the substance of the same discourse? What, then, in the case supposed, would be the result? Socrates would have four *memorabilia*, or records of his memorable deeds, for each of which, in virtue of his revisal of them all, he would be as thoroughly responsible, down to the very sentences and syllables, as if he had himself written it with his own proper hand; while each, again, would preserve the freshness and naturalness of its own separate authorship; and the whole together would carry the full force of four independent testimonies to the credit of the life which Socrates actually led, and the doctrines which Socrates taught.

The case is really the same, so far as the consideration now in question is concerned, whether it be verbal revisal afterwards, or verbal inspiration beforehand. The Spirit is as much at liberty to dictate and direct the writing of four different accounts of Christ's ministry, according to the different minds and memories of the compilers whom he employs, as Socrates would be to sanction four different reports of his teaching, taken down by four of his followers of very various capacities and tastes, and submitted for his *imprimatur* to himself. An exact agreement in accounts given by different persons of things done or said, is not essential to the integrity of the narrators; it would often be a proof of preconcerted fraud. Neither is it essential to the integrity of one revising their several accounts;—even if he do so under the condition of becoming himself accountable, as much as if he were directly the author, for every one of them, and for everything that is in every one of them. It cannot, therefore, be fairly regarded as inconsistent with the integrity of the Holy Spirit, that, in inspiring the four evangelical narratives, he should give to each the impression of its own characteristic authorship; so as to make them severally tell as distinct attestations, upon the faith of independent witnesses, to the things that were said and done by the Lord Jesus in Galilee and in Judæa.

But again, for the purposes of life, and interest, and spirit, as well as for the purposes of evidence, the arrangement in question is important. The Bible would have been comparatively tame and dull, if it had come to us as the utterance of an angelic voice, or as all at once engraven on a table of stone. Its power over us largely depends upon its being the voice of humanity, as well as the voice of Deity; and upon its being the voice, moreover, of our common humanity, expressing itself in accommodation to all the varieties of age, language, situation, and modes of thought, by which our common humanity is modified. A stiff thing, indeed, would the Revelation of God have been if it had been proclaimed once, or twice, or ever so often, by an oracular response from a Sybil's cave, or by a heavenly trumpet pealing articulate words in the startled ear. God has wisely and graciously ordered it otherwise. He inspires men to speak to men—he inspires men to write for men. And he inspires men of all sorts; living in various times and countries; occupying various positions; accustomed to various styles. He inspires them, moreover, as they are,—as he finds them. He does not put them all into one Procrustes-bed of forced uniformity. He uses them freely, according to their several peculiarities. They are all his instruments; but they are his instruments according to their several natures, and the circumstances in which they are severally placed. Every word they write is his; but he makes it his, by guiding them to the use of it as their own.

Doubtless there is some difficulty in our thus conceiving of this divine work. But it is not a difficulty that need affect either our understanding of the Spirit's meaning, or our recognition of his one agency throughout, amid all the diversities of composition which he may see fit to employ.

Thus, as to the first of these points, with reference to our understanding the Spirit's meaning when he thus variously inspires the various writers of the Bible, we must apply the same sagacity that we would bring to bear upon the miscellaneous writings of a human author. A mass of papers, written or dictated by a friend, or a father, comes into my hands. They are of a very miscellaneous character, with a great variety of dates, ranging over many years of time, and almost every clime and country of the globe. They consist of all manner of compositions, in prose and poetry,—historical pieces,—letters on all sorts of subjects, and to all sorts of people,—antiquarian researches,—tales of fiction,—with verses in abundance, lyric, dramatic, didactic, and devotional. I receive the precious legacy, and I apply my reason to estimate and arrange so welcome an "*embarras des richesses.*" And here there are two distinct questions; the first, What can I legitimately gather out of the materials before me as to the real mind of the author on any given subject? and the second, What weight is due to his opinion or authority? Assuming this last question to be settled—and it is the fair assumption—what remains as to the first? There may be very considerable difficulty in dealing with it, and much room for the exercise, and, let it be added emphatically, for the trial of my candour, patience, and good faith. There is not a little confusion, let us say, in the mass of materials to be disposed of; it needs to be examined, assorted, and classified. There may be room for inquiry, in particular instances, as to how far, and in what manner, the author means to express his own views in his narratives and stories, or in his poetical productions, or even in his abrupt, off-hand, and occasionally rhetorical reasoning. There may be need of a certain large-minded and large-hearted shrewdness, far removed from that of the mere "word-catcher that lives on syllables," and able to enter into the genuine earnestness with which the writer throws himself always into the scenes and the circumstances before him,—nay, even when he employs an amanuensis, into the habits of thought, and the very manner of expression, of his scribe. The voluminous and varied papers of more than one great man might furnish an example of what I mean.

Now, in a sense quite analogous to this, the Bible may be said to consist of the papers of God himself. They are very miscellaneous papers: every sort of character is personated, as it were, in the preparation of them; every different style of writing is employed; every age is represented, and every calling. There are treatises of all sorts, which must be interpreted according to their respective rules of composition. And yet an intelligent reader can discriminate between the several discoveries which God makes of himself,—in the inspired history of the Pentateuch, in the inspired drama of Job, in the inspired reports of Christ's own teaching, in the inspired reasoning of Paul's epistles,—just as accurately as he can gather a human author's real sentiments upon any point from a comparison of his different writings—the plays, and poems, and tales, and histories, and treatises, and sermons, which he may have composed. His mind is not indicated in the same way in each and all of these various kinds of writing. It is discovered more directly in some, and more inferentially in others. Still, they are all his writings; he is responsible for every word of every one of them; and, taken freely and fairly together, they authentically, and with sufficient clearness and certainty, declare his views.

Nor again, on the other hand, need we have any serious difficulty in recognising the one divine agency that pervades the various compositions which the Bible comprehends within itself.

Let it be assumed that God means to compose a book, such as shall at once bear the stamp of his own infallible authority, and have enough of human interest to carry our sympathies along with it. He may accomplish this by a miracle in a moment; the book may drop suddenly complete from heaven; and sufficient proofs and signs may attest the fact. Even in that case, unless the miracle is to be perpetual, the book once launched has the usual hazards of time and chance to run in the world; in the process of endless copying and printing, it is liable to the usual literary accidents; and in the course of centuries, sundry points of criticism emerge regarding it. But instead of thus issuing the volume at once and entire from above, its divine Author chooses to compile it more gradually on the earth, and he chooses also to avail himself of the command which he has of the mind and tongue and pen of every man that lives. He selects, accordingly, chosen men from age to age. These he does not turn into machines; they continue to be men. They speak and write according to their individual tastes and temperaments, in all the various departments of literary composition: the prince, the peasant, the publican, the learned scribe, the unlettered child of toil, one skilled in all the wisdom of Egypt, another bred among the herdmen of Tekoa,—men, too, of all variety of natural endowments, the rapt poet, the ripe scholar, the keen reasoner, the rude annalist and bare chronicler of events, the dry and tedious compiler, if you will,—all are enlisted in the service, and the Divine Spirit undertakes so to penetrate their minds and hearts, and so to guide them in the very utterance and recording of their sentiments, as to make what they say and write, when under his inspiration, the word of God in a sense not less exact than if, with his own finger, he had graven it on the sides of the everlasting hills.

Many questions, doubtless, will arise to exercise the skill and tact of readers, and put their intelligence and good faith to the test; for it is to intelligence and good faith that this volume of miscellanies is committed. In the case of any author writing freely and naturally, it often becomes a nice point of criticism to determine how far and in what way he is to be held as giving any opinion of his own; as, for example, when he narrates the speeches and actions of others, or when in an abrupt play of argumentative wit he mixes up the adversary's pleas with his own, or when he uses parables and figures, or when he adapts himself to the state of information and measure of aptitude to learn among those for whom he writes, or when he writes in different characters and for different ends. On the principle of plenary inspiration, it is of course assumed that the same sagacity and good sense will be applied to those various works of which God is thus the author, that we do not grudge in a case of voluminous and versatile human authorship; and it is confessed that the whole inquiry regarding the books to be included in the collected edition of these works, the purity and accuracy of the text, and the rules of sound literal interpretation, falls within the province of the uninspired understanding of mankind, and must be disposed of according to the light which the testimony of the Church, the literary history of the canon, and other sources of information may afford.

But what then? Does this detract from the value of our having an infallible communication from the divine mind,—somewhat fragmentary, if you will, and manifold, having been made "at sundry times and in divers manners," πολυμερῶς και πολυτρόπως,—but still conveying to us, on divine authority, and with a divine guarantee for its perfect accuracy, the knowledge of the character and ways of God, the history of redemption, the plan of salvation, the message of grace, and the hope of glory? Or does it hinder the assurance which, under the teaching of the Holy Ghost, a plain man may have, as the Scriptures enter into his mind, carrying their own light and evidence along with them, that he has God speaking to him as unequivocally as one friend speaks to another,—but with an authority all his own?

I have dwelt so long upon my first topic—which is the preliminary work of clearing the way—that I must hasten rapidly over the remainder of the ground. In particular I must dismiss, almost without remark, the second and third branches of the subject,—the method of proof, and the sources of difficulty. This I do the more willingly, because they are found sufficiently discussed in many excellent and easily accessible treatises, and because the principles upon which they are discussed in these treatises are really not substantially affected by those transcendental speculations, which threaten to involve the whole question of a divine test or standard of truth in hopeless and inextricable confusion.

II. In regard to the method of proof—I may briefly indicate the line of evidence that seems most simple and satisfactory; only premising again that we must assume, at this stage, an acquiescence in the truth of Christianity, as well as in the genuineness of its books as historical and literary documents.

1. First, then, I start with the undoubted fact, that Jesus and his apostles recognised the Old Testament Scriptures as of divine authority, and divinely inspired. This is clear from the use which they made of them in their discourses and writings.

It must be remembered that, in our Lord's day, the sacred books of the Jews existed, not as miscellaneous works of different authors, having different claims upon men's attention and belief, but as one volume, of which throughout God was held to be the author. The contents of the volume were well defined. It had its well-known division into three parts. But it was always freely quoted and referred to as one complete whole; and the words contained in it anywhere, in any of its parts, were always cited as divine. I do not here inquire into the formation of the Jewish canon. That is a matter of history involved in much obscurity. When, how, and by whom, the writings of Moses and the Prophets were collected, revised, and published as one book—by what authority and under what guidance—we may be unable to ascertain. But that does not affect the notorious fact that the book did exist, as one book, in our Lord's day; and that it was so well known as having the character of a peculiar, a sacred book, that any allusion made to it by him and his apostles could admit of no misapprehension.

Now, whenever either he, or they, do allude to that book, or any portion of it, it is in language implying in the strongest manner its divine authority and inspiration. Such phrases as, "It is written"—"Well spake the Holy Ghost by the mouth of" such a one—"The Scripture saith"—"David in the Spirit calleth him Lord"—these and similar forms of expression will readily occur; together with such exhortations and testimonies, as "Search the Scriptures"—"Then began he to open up to them the Scriptures, and to show that Christ must needs have suffered, and have risen from the dead"—"These were more noble than the men of Thessalonica, in that they searched the Scriptures daily whether these things were so." The uniform manner of speaking of the Old Testament which we trace in the sayings and writings of Christ and his apostles in the New—is such as to be wholly incompatible with any other idea than that of its full and verbal inspiration: and cannot but convey to a simple reader the impression that they regarded every word of that Testament as divine.

2. There are manifest traces, in the teaching of Christ and his apostles, of the design to have a volume, and of the actual forming of a volume, under the New Dispensation, corresponding in respect of autho-

rity and inspiration to that existing under the Old, and equally entitled to the name of the Scriptures, or the Word of God. Not to speak of the presumption that this really would be the case—since surely God could not be expected to provide less security for the gospel being infallibly transmitted among the families of men, than for the law being so transmitted—and not to dwell on the plain intimations which Christ gave of his design to have his own words perpetuated upon earth, and to endow his apostles with the gift of the Holy Spirit, for the utterance, as well as for the understanding, of all truth,—it is impossible to read the epistles generally, without perceiving that we have in them the gradual compiling of books that are to lay just claim to a place in the New Testament volume. And in particular, it is impossible to evade the force of the Apostle Peter's testimony, classing the writings of his brother Apostle Paul among the well-known Scriptures—as to whose divine character there could be no doubt.[1]

Here, again, we may be at a loss to explain, historically, the settlement of the Christian canon. This much, however, seems plain enough. The early Christians had every reason to believe and be sure that inspired narratives of gospel history, and treatises on gospel truth, would be forthcoming. And when called to discriminate between these and other publications, they were in the

[1] "And account that the long suffering of our Lord is salvation; even as our beloved brother Paul also, according to the wisdom given unto him, hath written unto you; as also in all his epistles, speaking in them of these things: in which are some things hard to be understood, which they that are unlearned and unstable wrest, as they do also the other scriptures, unto their own destruction."—2 Pet. iii. 15, 16.

best possible circumstances for knowing and judging what were divine and what were not. That they were, in point of fact, guided to a wonderfully correct discrimination, must be evident to every one who considers the cautious pains which they took, and the scrupulous jealousy which they exercised, in admitting books into the canon;—especially when in connection with that, he compares the books actually admitted, with those of the like kind discarded or rejected. The contrast is so striking between the most doubtful of the canonical books and the very best of the apocryphal, or the patristic, in point of doctrine, sentiment, taste, sense, and judgment—that scarcely any one can hesitate to admit that the early Christians came to a sound conclusion when they recognised the present set of works as composing the New Testament Scriptures—which they had already been led beforehand to expect, and which they had been taught to place upon the same level, in point of inspiration and authority, with the Old Testament Scriptures themselves, as the Jews had been wont to accept them.

3. And now, at this stage, we are fully warranted in applying to the books, both of the Old and New Testaments, viewed as a whole, whatever testimonies we find anywhere in the Bible to the plenary character of the inspiration of Scripture. Among others, including the familiar formulæ of quotation already noticed—two in particular stand out; the first, that of the Apostle Paul (2 Tim. iii. 16)—"All scripture is given by inspiration of God;" and the second, that of the Apostle Peter (2 Pet. i. 20, 21)—"No prophecy of the scripture is of

any private interpretation. For the prophecy came not in old time by the will of man: but holy men of God spake as they were moved by the Holy Ghost."

In the first of these passages, inspiration is plainly ascribed to Scripture or to the written word;—not to the conception of divine things in the mind, but to the writing down of divine things with the pen. In so far as inspiration can be predicated of any scripture or writing at all, it must, according to this testimony, be inspiration reaching to the very words or language, as written down.

The other passage, again, giving the reason why no prophecy, or no revelation, of Scripture is of any private interpretation, uses phraseology singularly explicit and strong: "Holy men of God spake as they were moved by the Holy Ghost." And the argument implied is a striking confirmation of this view. It is briefly this. No human author should have his meaning judged of by any single, isolated observation or expression, in some one portion of his works. You are not at liberty to fasten upon a single sentence, as if it must needs be exclusively its own interpreter, and as if out of it alone you were to gather the author's mind on any point at issue. He is entitled to the benefit of being allowed to explain himself; and you are bound to ascertain his views, not by forcing one solitary passage to interpret itself, but by comparing it with other passages, and from a fair survey of the scope and tenor of his whole writings, collecting what he really means to teach. The Author of the Bible, argues the apostle, has a right to the same mode of treatment. If, indeed, each holy man of God had spoken simply by his own "will," then the Bible would have many authors, and each author must speak for himself; his teaching, apart from that of others, must be self-interpreting. But if holy men of God spake as they were moved by the Holy Ghost, then the Bible has really but one author—the Holy Ghost. And in dealing with it, you are to deal with it as one whole,—the product of one mind—the collection of the miscellaneous works of one divine Author.[1]

4. Finally, to a mind rightly exercised upon them, and above all, to a heart influenced by the same Holy Spirit who breathes in them, the Scriptures evidence themselves to be of divine authority and divine inspiration. This is a great and glorious theme, upon which, however, it is impossible, in the present lecture, to expatiate or enlarge. One remark only I would make, in reference to a somewhat unfair objection that has been raised against this branch of the proof of inspiration. It is admitted that some books and passages of the Bible do commend themselves to the honest mind and pious heart as divine. But what impress of divinity does any one feel or own in the genealogies of Matthew and Luke, or in the dry catalogue of names in the tenth chapter of Nehemiah? The question is almost too absurd to deserve a reply; and yet very spiritual and transcendental philosophers have condescended to put it. If it is anything more, in any instance, than a mere trick of argument, a poor

[1] See, for some further use of this text, the succeeding Lecture on the Infallibility of the Bible.

and paltry hit,—if any one is seriously embarrassed by it,—a plain natural analogy may furnish a satisfactory reply.

My child feels the letter which I write to him to be from me. He lovingly recognises my spirit breathing in it, and prompting all the words of simple fatherly fondness that I address to him. "It is my father's letter, all through," he cries;—"I trace my father's warm and loving heart in every syllable of it." My own actual hand-writing may not be on the page: sickness, or some casualty, may have made an amanuensis necessary. But my boy knows my letter nevertheless—knows it as all my own—knows it by the instinct, the intuition of affection, and needs no other proof. And what would he say to any cold, cynical, hypercritical schoolmates, who might ask,—But what of your father do you discern in that barren itinerary with which the letter begins—the dry list of places he tells you he has gone through; or in that matter-of-course message about a cloak and some books with which it ends? How would he resent the foolish impertinence! How would he grasp the precious document all the more tightly, and clasp it all the closer to his bosom! "You may be too knowing to sympathise with me," he will reply;—"but there is enough in every line here to make me know my father's voice; and if he has been at the pains to write down for my satisfaction the names of towns and cities and men—if he does give me simple notices about common things, I see nothing strange in that. I love him all the better for his kindness and condescension; and whatever you may insinuate, I will believe that this is all throughout his very letter, and that he has a gracious meaning in all that he writes to me in it, however frivolous it may seem to you."

III. The sources of difficulty, in connection with this subject, are many; nor is it wonderful that it should be so, and that the lapse of time, and the loss of nearly all contemporary information, should render the solution of some perplexing questions impossible. There is much that is incomprehensible in the doctrine, or fact, of inspiration itself, and not a few things in the inspired Scriptures confessedly hard to be understood. Objectors are fond of multiplying and magnifying these difficulties,—drawing them out in long and formidable array, and giving them all the pomp and circumstance of successive numerical enumeration. In point of fact there are two classes to which they may all be reduced.

1. There are critical difficulties connected with the canon, the original text, the translations, and the interpretation of the Scriptures. Several elements of uncertainty are thus introduced which, it is alleged, go far to neutralise the benefit of an infallible, plenary inspiration.

Now it is admitted, of course, *first* that the question of the canon,—what books are to be received as of divine authority, or what books do the Scriptures contain,—is mainly a question of human learning—*secondly*, that the original text of the sacred books has suffered from successive copyings, that it must be adjusted by a comparison of manuscripts, and that the best adjustment can furnish only an approximation to absolute accuracy—*thirdly*, that all translations, ancient and modern, are imperfect—and, *fourthly,* that the ordinary rules of criticism must be applied to the interpretation of the Bible, and that in applying them there may be doubt, hesitancy, and error. It is confessed that these circumstances do imply that a certain measure of uncertainty attaches to the Scriptures as we now have them; though far less than in the case of any other ancient book, as facts prove, and as there are obvious reasons to explain. But what of that? Because we, at this distance of time and place, can have but a transcript, somewhat marred and obscured by the wear and tear of ages, of the inspired volume as it originally, in its several parts, came directly from God,—does it therefore follow that there was no inspiration of the original books at all? Or that we would have been as well off if there had been none?

The strangest perversion of mind appears among our opponents upon this point. One learned Theban, for instance, a profound Anglican divine,[1] objects to our view of inspiration, on the ground that it precludes the application of criticism to the settlement of the text, or the interpretation of the meaning of the Bible. I would have imagined it to have an exactly opposite tendency. If the Scriptures have God as their author, it surely concerns us all the more on that account, to have them submitted to the most searching critical scrutiny. What pains do critics take with the remains of a favourite

[1] See "Vindication of Protestant Principles," by "Phileleutherus Anglicanus,"—that is, as is well known, Dr. Donaldson, late head-master of Bury St. Edmund's School, and author of the "New Craylus," and other more recent publications in which his views on the subject of this lecture, and on other kindred subjects, are brought out in still more marked opposition to the received opinions of the churches of Christendom.

classic! With what zeal will a Bentley apply himself to the works of Horace; first, to see to it that no spurious production is allowed to pass under that honoured name; secondly, to make the text, by a comparison of manuscripts, and the exercise of a sound, critical acumen, as nearly as possible, immaculately accurate; thirdly, to guard against mistakes in translation; and, fourthly, to lay down the rules, and catch the spirit, that may enable him most thoroughly to enter into and draw out his loved author's meaning! In all these particulars the pains spent upon the works of Horace may with tenfold more reason be spent upon the word of God. And the more thoroughly and completely the Scriptures are held to be the very word of God, so much the more need will there be for the vocation of the sound biblical critic. Our worthy scholar and theologian, therefore, may calm his alarmed soul, and rest assured that the theory of a plenary inspiration will give him no cause to cry "Othello's occupation's gone!"

2. The other class of difficulties are of a historical, physical, and moral, rather than of a critical, kind; consisting of alleged inconsistencies and contradictions, whether between different passages of the Bible themselves, or between the Bible and the facts of history, or the laws of nature. These would require to be dealt with in detail; and this cannot be attempted at the end of so long a lecture. But one general observation may be suggested. No intelligent defender of plenary inspiration need be ashamed to own that, in many instances, he cannot reconcile apparent disagreements. For, after all, the Scriptures are fragmentary writings: and we would

require to have far fuller information on all the matters of which they treat, to enable us to say which of several possible explanations may be the right one, or whether there may not be an explanation in reserve, such as our limited knowledge fails to suggest to us.

IV. But I must now close with a brief reference to my fourth and last topic. I would vindicate, in a few words, this sacred doctrine of the authority and inspiration of the Bible, against the charge of Bibliolatry, rashly vented, in an evil hour, by a man too great for the use of such a nickname; and eagerly bandied about by a whole tribe of lesser followers, to the exposure of their own conceit, as much as to the scandal of pious minds.

"Bibliolatry!" "Mechanical Inspiration!" "As of a drawer receiving what is put in it!" "Cabalistic Ventriloquism!" So the pleasant sarcasm takes! And the ingenuity of sucessive lovers of freedom is taxed, as they go on improving on one another! One of the most recent improvements, perhaps, is due to Professor Sherer, formerly of Geneva, to whom belongs the credit of that inimitably happy hit, "Cabalistic Ventriloquism!"

What profanity, one is inclined to exclaim! And yet, need we wonder? It is not meant for profanity by the writers. Nay, they think they are doing God service. And they do well to get a convenient by-word, or term of reproach, that may make short work with Christ's word, —as certain men of old contrived by such a by-word,— or by two,—blasphemy and treason,—to make short work with Christ's person.

But we wrong them. They are the champions of liberty. They are to emancipate the soul from the Protestant yoke of subjection to the Bible, as well as from the popish yoke of submission to the church. Authority, —especially authority claiming to be infallible,—must be set aside; and man must be absolutely free! The Papist has his church. The Protestant has his Bible. Both are almost equally bad. For me, I have as the object of my faith, the person of Jesus Christ! And ask me not to define who, or what, Jesus Christ is. Far less ask me to define what his work was upon the earth. All the ills of Christianity come from definition. Let me have the person of Jesus Christ, as my intuitional consciousness, quickened by a divine inspiration of it, apprehends him; let me lose myself in him: let me plunge into the infinite divine love of which he is the impersonation.

But I cannot pretend to make intelligible the rhapsodies of this new anti-biblical mysticism. Nor need I dwell on the approaches to it that are but too discernible in the whole school that would substitute what is called "the Christian consciousness" for the direct authority of Scripture. Let it suffice to contrast man's position before God, upon the true Protestant footing of his owning the Scriptures as authoritative and inspired, with either of the other two positions which he may be regarded as occupying;—when, on the one hand, he rejects, more or less, their inspired authority, or when he substitutes for them, on the other hand, the authority of church or Pope.

1. Some would have it that Christianity is purely a subjective influence on the minds of men—that the gos-

pel operates by assimilating the soul to itself—that Christ is not a revealer, but a revelation—and that as the central revelation of God, he becomes the occasion, or the means, through the working of the Spirit, of our intuitively apprehending God, and being renewed into his likeness. According to this view, God brings to bear upon you a series and succession of influences, partly external and partly internal, fitted to emancipate you from corruption, and elevate you to a participation in the divine nature. It is a subjective process,—a working in and upon you, so that like the plastic clay, you take the impress and character into which you are moulded; and the Scriptures, as an exhibition of God in Christ, have an important part in the process. But in all this, there is nothing like God addressing himself directly to you, and dealing with you, as it were, face to face. There is no real, objective transaction or negotiation of peace between you and him. This, however, is the very peculiarity of the gospel, as we conceive of it; that God not merely influences man, but speaks to man. He treats man, not as a creature merely, but as a subject; not merely as a creature needing to be renovated, but as a subject to be called to account.

The two systems are directly conflicting here. And which, think you, best consults in the long-run for the true dignity and liberty of man?

Tell me that I am brought within the range of influences and impulses, inward revelations and spiritual operations of various kinds, to be grasped by my intuitional consciousness, and to be available, through the exercise of my soul upon them, and their hold over me, for my regeneration. In one view, my pride may be gratified. These divine communications are all subject to me: I am their master: I receive them only in so far as they commend themselves to my acceptance: and I use and wield them for my own good. But after all, in the whole of this process, am I not passive, rather than active? It is God acting upon me; according to my intelligent and self-conscious nature, no doubt; but still very much as if he were acting upon some sort of substance that is to be sublimated into an ethereal essence, and is to lose itself ultimately in the surrounding air.

But tell me that God has something objectively to say to me,—that he summons me as a responsible, and in a sense, an independent being before him,—that he treats with me upon terms that recognise my standing at his bar,—that he calls me to account,—that he reckons with me for my sin,—that he directs me to a surety,—that he makes proposals of mercy,—that he puts it into my heart to comply with these proposals,—that I, personally, and face to face, come to an understanding with him personally, and that he, judicially acquitting me, receives me as a loyal subject, a son, an heir, and works in me both to will and to do, while I work out my own salvation with fear and trembling. Tell me all this, and tell me further, that the charter of this real and actual negotiation of peace is in his word, as the Scriptures infallibly record it. And then judge ye, if I am not really made to occupy a far loftier, nobler, freer position in the presence of my God, than the highest possible refinement of subjective illumination and transformation could ever of itself reach?

It is true in this instance, as it is true universally, that "whosoever humbleth himself shall be exalted." Refusing to submit yourself to the divine word, you may affect a superiority over the slaves of mere authority: and you may work yourself into a state of ideal absorption into Christ, little different in reality from the pantheistic dream of a rapturous absorption into the great mundane intelligence. But yield an implicit deference to the word. Let it absolutely and unreservedly rule you, as a real objective communication of his mind, by God, to you. Then you have realities to deal with. You have real sin, and a real sentence of death;—a real atonement, a real justification, a real adoption;—a real portion in the favour of God now, a real work of progressive sanctification, and a real inheritance in heaven at last.

2. Nor let us be greatly moved, even if it shall be alleged against us that our reverence for the Bible is to be placed on the same level with the Romanist's blind obedience to the Church, and the Church's head upon earth. In point of fact, no tendency towards the recognition of an infallible human authority can be more direct and strong than that which the denial of an infallible objective standard of divine truth implies. Set aside the Scriptures as not furnishing such a standard. You are thrown back either on the individual intuition of each believer, or on the Christian consciousness of the general community of believers. But neither of these refuges will long satisfy or soothe an earnest soul. Soon there will come to be felt a sad want of some surer prop. And whether as relieving the individual from his undefined

responsibility, or as giving shape and power to the indefinite notion of a general Christian consciousness,—an ecclesiastical voice will be allowed to speak as the interpreter of the dumb mind of Christendom; and the weary spirit will sink to rest, and find its home, in the maternal embrace of Rome.

But apart from this consideration, an emphatic protest must be uttered against the attempt to represent the Scriptures in Protestantism, as occupying a parallel position to that of the Church in Mediævalism;—or to that of the Pope in Romanism.

The real truth is, that the Pope,—and the same may be said of the Church,—does not take the place of the Bible. He usurps the throne of Him whom the Bible elevates as the only High Priest and King in Zion;—Christ Jesus the Lord. He assumes the office of Him who alone interprets authoritatively the Scriptures which he has inspired;—the Holy Ghost, the Great Teacher of the Church. And the glory of Protestantism is not that it puts the Bible instead of the Pope, but that it puts Christ instead of the Pope, as the great object of the Bible's testimony, and the Spirit instead of the Pope, as the Bible's only interpreter. The Bible—the Bible alone, is the religion of Protestants; the Bible, not sealed under the papal key, and doled out by the papal ministers;—but the Bible left freely in the hands of its Divine Author, the Holy Ghost, to be by Him freely opened up to every devout and serious child of man, that he may know him who is the only true God, and Jesus Christ whom he has sent;—whom to know is life eternal.

THE INFALLIBILITY

OF

HOLY SCRIPTURE.

THE

INFALLIBILITY OF HOLY SCRIPTURE.

I THINK it right to explain at the outset of my lecture, that I do not intend to traverse the whole field of inquiry which the question of the inspiration of Scripture opens up. The principles and rules according to which the canon of Scripture should be settled, and the genuineness and authenticity of its several books should be ascertained, I cannot even notice. Nor do I touch upon such topics as the methods of verifying and correcting, by the collation of manuscripts, the original inspired text; or the use and value of translations. All these points may have a bearing on the question, and must be embraced in any full discussion of it. But they do not enter into its essential merits. I must add that I do not mean even to attempt anything like the leading of proof, external or internal, in behalf of the plenary inspiration or infallibility of the Bible. All that I propose to myself in a lecture like this, is to try my hand at an adjustment, or what may contribute to an adjustment, of the state of the question; to bring out what it is that the advocates of this doctrine really hold, and to bring out also the qualifications and conditions under which they hold it. Much is gained if I succeed in clearing up our position, and contribute any help towards the extrication of it from the confusion in which irrelevant discussions of matters altogether beside the point have, as one is sometimes tempted to think, almost hopelessly involved it.

According to the plan and method of my present investigation, I do not care much about any definition of terms. Such definition of terms would be indispensable, if I were about to enter into the whole subject methodically and comprehensively; but, so far as my present object is concerned, I hope to be able to accomplish it without the aid of rigid formal and scholastic technicality. I am content to understand by revelation whatever God has to say to man, whether man might have discovered it for himself or not; and as to inspiration, I care for no admission or acknowledgment of it which does not imply infallibility. I intend, indeed, rather to avoid the use of this word inspiration; not because I consider it unsuitable—it is the right word—but because it has been, I fear I must say disingenuously, perverted from its recognised meaning, as expressive of that divine superintendence of the process of revelation which secures infallibly the truth and accuracy of what is revealed, and made to signify the mere elevation, more or less, of human, and therefore fallible, capacity or faculty.

Briefly I intend, first, to offer two preliminary remarks in explanation of what, as I understand it, is meant when the infallibility of the Bible is asserted; and then to indicate some of the conditions—four of them—under which that assertion of the infallibility of the Bible is made.

First, then, I have to offer two preliminary remarks in explanation of what is meant when the infallibility of the Bible is asserted. The first has respect to the nature, the second to the extent, of the infallibility claimed.

1. By the infallibility of the Bible, I simply mean that it is the infallible record of an infallible revelation. The infallibility is purely and simply objective. It is the attribute of the revelation and of the record, viewed altogether apart from the interpretation which each may receive, and the impression which it may make, in the subjective mind with which it comes in contact. The revelation, as given by God, is infallible; it may not be so, as apprehended by men. The record of it, as prompted or superintended by God, is infallible; it may not be so, as read by us.

It may seem unnecessary to advert to so plain and obvious a distinction. But those who are familiar with certain recent modes of reasoning on inspiration, are aware that not a little pains has been taken, by mixing up and confounding things which differ, to wrap the whole subject of revelation, and the record of revelation, in a sort of dim and doubtful mist.

Thus, as to revelation, the divine influence under which Moses spoke when he gave the law; Isaiah, when he described beforehand the sufferings of Christ; Paul, when he taught the doctrine of grace—is represented as differing from the divine influence under which a good and gifted man speaks now, when he discourses on the law, on Christ, on grace; not generically, or in kind, but in amount, or quantity, or degree. Hence it has been inferred that, however much their insight into these matters may have been clearer, higher, more intuitive, more far-reaching in all directions—above, beneath, behind, before—than that of others who have had less of the co-operation of the Spirit, it cannot amount to absolute and complete certainty. It may be far more trustworthy and satisfying, but it is not infallible.

So, also, as to the record of revelation, the Apostle John, writing his Master's life, enjoys a larger measure of divine influence and guidance than an ordinary biographer recording the sayings and doings of a pious friend. But it is an influence and guidance of the same nature. It enabled "the disciple whom Jesus loved" better to understand the divine subject of his memoir, to enter with deeper sympathy into his Master's mind and heart, and therefore to give a better and more vivid picture of him, as well as a more exact transcript of his teaching, than he could otherwise have done. Still, even John might fail to grasp the whole bearings, the full and exact significancy, of the story which he had to tell; and so, in the telling of it, he may have come short of the truth, or unawares, occasionally, misrepresented it.

Now, the fallacy of all this seems to lie in not distinguishing the position of one through whom a revelation is given, or by whom it is recorded, from the position of an ordinary person attending to the revelation, or reading the record. The question is not, Was Isaiah's knowledge of the message which he had to deliver full and infallible? but, Did God see to it, and make sure, that by means of Isaiah's instrumentality the message should be fully and infallibly communicated to those to whom he ministered?

It is not, Was there in the prophet himself infallibility? but, Was there infallibility in his prophetic teaching? So far as concerns his own understanding of what God commissioned him to reveal, he might be in the same position with any other member of the Church—more enlightened, certainly, but not necessarily infallible. God is the revealer—not Isaiah. The infallibility, therefore, lies in the disclosure or discovery which God causes the prophet to make—not in the insight of the prophet himself. This is the view suggested by the Apostle Peter :—" Of which salvation the prophets have inquired and searched diligently, who prophesied of the grace that should come unto you: searching what, or what manner of time, the Spirit of Christ which was in them did signify, when it testified beforehand the sufferings of Christ, and the glory that should follow. Unto whom it was revealed, that not unto themselves, but unto us, they did minister the things which are now reported unto you by them that have preached the gospel unto you with the Holy Ghost sent down from heaven; which things the angels desire to look into" (1 Peter i. 10-12).

Take also the record of a revelation; and, to simplify the matter, let it again be the Evangelist John, writing down one of the discourses of the Lord Jesus, in which it will be admitted, that when Jesus delivered it, there was an infallible revelation. As regards his own apprehension and hold of the discourse, John in writing it may be regarded as similarly situated with us in reading it;—with immensely greater advantages no doubt for taking it all accurately in, but still, in that personal point of view, not necessarily infallible—not fully and infallibly enlightened. And yet the infallibility of the record which he pens may be secured by the immediate oversight of the infallible Spirit.

2. Such being the nature of the infallibility claimed,—let us now consider its extent.

All that is in Scripture is not revelation. To a large extent the Bible is a record of human affairs—the sayings and doings of men, not always a record of divine doctrine, or of communications from God. Is it infallible when it narrates the wars of kings, and inserts the genealogies of tribes and families;—as strictly so as when it reports an immediate oracle of Heaven, or embodies the religious teaching of prophets and apostles?

To determine this point, in so far as the necessity of the case may be allowed to bear upon it, let the actual plan and method of the revelation which the Bible records be briefly considered. How, in point of fact, has it pleased God to reveal his will to man?

I can imagine his doing so in a form and manner that would admit of easy extrication from the events of history and the actions of men. All that he intended to say to the human race—the whole instruction which he wished to give them verbally by direct discovery from himself, apart from what they might otherwise gather from his works and ways—might have been comprised in one single communication, made all at once, and once for all, to one competent person, or simultaneously to a select number, associated for the purpose. That one communication might have been complete in itself, embracing whatever information and direction God meant in this way to afford for the guidance of mankind in all ages.

Let us suppose the original parents of the race to have been in possession of this one communication—to have got such an authentic revelation—clearly and unequivocally certified to their own minds to be no discovery of theirs, but a direct communication of God—his very word spoken in their ears. Let us further suppose that they made, or received, a record of this communication, and that the document has come down in tolerable preservation to the present day. On this supposition it is quite conceivable that books similar to those of which the Bible is composed might be written from age to age; breaking up the one original and complete revelation into its constituent parts and elements; applying these, in orderly or miscellaneous detail, to the several exigencies of history,—whether the history of the entire race, or that of particular families, or nations, or individuals:—and showing the different uses made of them, "at sundry times and in divers manners," by the leading minds of successive generations. The primeval divine communication might thus, as it were, be reproduced bit by bit in the writings of men prompted, under the ordinary divine influence vouchsafed to holy men, to illustrate and unfold its various bearings, at manifold points of contact, on the progress of human society, the conditions of human life, and the experiences of the human heart. There might be books of history, legislation, poetry, devotion, and in a sense, also, prophecy; didactic treatises, familiar letters, songs, proverbs, parables;—all based upon the old revelation, pervaded by its spirit, drawing out its principles into their practical issues, and so interspersed with its very words and phrases, its sentences and paragraphs, that what existed at the beginning as a complete divine whole might all be found, in the form of detached portions and scattered fragments, in the body of human literature thus gathering and growing up around it. I say human literature—for the literature might be merely human; and so long as the original revelation, in its original record, was within reach, and might be consulted, there would be little or no difficulty in disentangling the divine from the human. Even in that case, however, the value and usefulness of the books, as books written to connect the divine ideal with the realities of the actual world, would be comparatively small, if the writers of them were not infallibly guided, and were consequently liable to err. And supposing the document itself, in which the revelation is recorded as a whole, to be lost, after the body of literature is held to be complete,—in which the whole of it exists, indeed, but exists dispersed, and mixed with other matter,—what then? We have the revelation still. But who shall tell us what it is? Or how may we find out what it is? For we have it only as subjected to merely human handling; broken up and spread through a vast variety of writings known to be more or less merely human; itself, indeed, continuing infallible as before; to be found, however, only in the compositions of men, confessedly fallible; found there, moreover, without marks of quotation, or any definite or distinct signs of discrimination of any sort between what is of God and what is theirs. And the better the books fulfil the end for which I have supposed them to be written—the more thoroughly their authors succeed in making their several compositions, of whatever kind, the living practical embodiments and expressions of revealed truth; in which it is variously acted out in harmonious accordance with its own various parts and phases; so much the greater will be the difficulty of extricating and disentangling the divine ore from its human bed. In fact, this difficulty might be so great as to drive one to the alternative of either abandoning the idea of an infallible revelation altogether, or accepting as infallible the books themselves in which alone, upon the hypothesis in question, the infallible revelation is now contained.

This is the very alternative forced upon us, with reference to the volume, or collection of writings, which we call the Bible. Have we in it an infallible divine revelation at all? Can we have such a revelation, divine and infallible, unless the character or attribute of infallibility belongs in the fullest sense to the record in which it is contained—unless the Giver of the revelation guarantees the accuracy of what the recorders of the revelation write? Can the infallible word of God be in the Bible, unless the Bible itself is the infallible Word of God?

The manner in which the authoritative will of God has been actually communicated or revealed to men, is very much the reverse, or converse, of that in which I have been supposing it to be communicated; and the contrast may be of use in guiding our inquiries and remarks under such heads as the following, touching the conditions under which the infallibility of the Bible is asserted :—I. Revelation was to be gradual and progressive, not immediately and at once complete. II. It was to be practical and pointed; springing out of the exigencies, and framed for the occasions, of ordinary human life and experience, from day to day, and from age to age; plastic, therefore, in its susceptibility of adaptation to human modes of thought and feeling; not rigidly stereotyped in a divine mould of absolute perfection. III. It was to be natural and free; not stiff and formal. IV. It was, nevertheless, to be throughout limited and restricted; not ranging over all the field of possible knowledge, but embracing only what concerns the moral government of God and the salvation of man. Under such conditions as these, let us assume an infallible revelation to be given, and an infallible record of it to be framed; and let us ask if that record would not present very much the appearance which the Bible, as we now have it, presents? Let us look at the Bible as a book composed under these conditions; and let us see if they do not, on the one hand, indicate the direction in which evidence of its inspiration and infallibility may be sought, and, on the other hand, suggest the sources from whence a probable solution of most of the difficulties of this subject may be derived. The first two of these conditions may be said to attach chiefly to the divine element in the composition of the Bible; the last two to the human.

I. What God had to communicate by revelation to man

was to be communicated, not all at once, but as it were piecemeal; gradually and progressively.

Now, in the first place, this consideration suggests a very strong reason why God should from the beginning, and all along, superintend most closely and minutely the committing of his communications to writing, so as to secure even the verbal accuracy of the record.

I am aware that this is a mode of reasoning about God in the use of which there is need of the greatest caution. To infer that God must have taken a certain course with reference to any matter, merely because to our judgment it seems the only course suitable to the circumstances of the case, is not often either reverential or safe. In the present instance, however, I cannot but think that the presumption is peculiarly strong.

He who sees the end from the beginning, and before whom all truth lies open, employs me, an ignorant and fallible man, to put on record, not the whole of what he means to say, but only a small, a very small part of it. He knows the relation of that part to the whole; but I do not. He can judge how the part can be so put that it shall be found ultimately to fit into the whole; but I cannot. Is it credible that he will leave it to me, writing a history, or a poem, or a letter, to bring in the portion of revelation which I have got from him just as I think fit, and choose my own way of introducing and expressing it, without satisfying himself that it is treated entirely according to his own mind? You would not, as a merchant, trust a clerk, unacquainted with all the interests of your vast business, to send a message for you about some one of them, having bearings, which you understand and he cannot, upon the business as a whole. You would ask to see the document before it was despatched, and you would correct its very language.

Again, secondly, the fact of the divine communications which the Bible has to record being partial, and in a sense, fragmentary in their character, may prepare us to expect a good deal of difficulty in harmoniously adjusting and combining them. At all events, it ought to be an argument for much more modesty in dealing with the Scriptures than is sometimes shown.

An author, especially a voluminous author, is placed at a great disadvantage when his views and sentiments on any important truth have to be gathered from a great variety of miscellaneous writings, composed long ago, and spread over a long series of years. Even with the most honest desire to ascertain his real mind, and do him full justice, you are often greatly at a loss and at fault. You cannot explain how he was led to speak in this particular way at one time, and in that other particular way at another time. You do not wish, however, to magnify apparent anomalies and inconsistencies. You have a firm persuasion that the great man whose works you are studying knew what he was about when he wrote them, and had fixed opinions to advocate, and a well-digested system to maintain. You examine patiently, and judge candidly. And if you do find passages really difficult, in which he seems to express himself on any question, or to have himself acted in any emergency, in a way that somewhat jars with his statements elsewhere and his conduct at other times, you are not surprised. You call to mind that you are ignorant of many particulars of local, temporary, personal, or relative significance which may have influenced him on such occasions, and which, if known, would show that there was only a just and wise adaptation to the necessities of the case; involving no change, or compromise, or concession. And as you esteem highly the author and his writings, you readily acquiesce even in a solution merely conjectural, if it offers anything approaching to a satisfactory vindication of his consistency. Such a mode of procedure is reasonable and fair. It is common sense. It is bare justice.

Now, the divine communications which the Bible professes to record extend, with large intervals, over centuries. Surely, in all fairness, the Bible which records them ought to be treated and judged in the manner which I have been attempting to describe.

This is probably what the Apostle Peter means in that remarkable passage, in which he unequivocally asserts the divine authorship of the prophetic books, or of the Scriptures generally, and assigns it as the reason of a general rule or canon of exposition: "No prophecy of the scripture is of any private interpretation. For the prophecy came not in old time by the will of man; but holy men of God spake as they were moved by the Holy Ghost" (2 Peter i. 20, 21). He is proving that the hope of the Lord's coming in power and glory is no "cunningly devised fable." He first insists on the fact of the Transfiguration. Even in the midst of his humiliation our Lord's glory was beheld. "We," James, John, and I, "were eye-witnesses of his majesty." We actually saw him as he is to be seen at his Second Advent. This, of itself, affords a strong presumption in favour of what we teach, when "we make known unto you the power and coming of our Lord Jesus Christ." But "the word of prophecy" is a still "surer" evidence: clearer, more explicit, and more direct. To that word—to the Scriptures containing it—the apostle refers his readers for proof of the doctrine which he is teaching. And, in doing so, he gives them a strong caution. They are to "know this first"—they are to keep it in view as a primary and capital principle of interpretation—that "no prophecy of Scripture is of any private interpretation."

The maxim thus announced has been variously explained; but, taken in connection with the reason assigned for it, I apprehend its meaning to be somewhat to the following effect. If the Scripture were a collection of separate and independent treatises, composed by different authors, then each treatise might be expected to contain within itself the means and materials of its own interpretation. We would count it enough, in that case, to let each writer explain himself. We would give him the benefit of collating or comparing the passages in his own book fitted to qualify or throw light on one another; but we would not consider it necessary to travel beyond what he himself had written, to ride the marches, as it were, or adjust the terms of agreement, between him and the other authors whose works happened to be bound up in the same volume. But the Bible is not such a miscellany. Properly speaking, it has but one author—the Holy Ghost

—throughout. All the books in it are of his composition. He is responsible for them all. And that being so, he is entitled to the same measure of justice at our hands which an ordinary writer may claim. We are to take his writings as a whole, and interpret them by the help of one another; by allowing them to shed light on one another; sometimes, perhaps, to limit and restrict one another's meaning, and at other times greatly to enhance and enlarge it. This is the correct view of the Bible as the Word of God. It is the work of one author; and of an author, let it be remembered, whose object it is not to declare his whole mind and will at once, but to let it come out only very gradually, in a sort of fragmentary way, bit by bit, in detached portions. He purposely at first, and for a long time, restrains himself; and of necessity leaves many things, especially in his earlier communications, unexplained. It ought not, therefore, to be matter of surprise to us, nor ought it to be felt as impeaching the infallibility of the Bible, when we find the dealings of God with men in the days of old, as the Bible records them, to be in some particulars such as, at this distance of time, we cannot have cleared up to our entire satisfaction. It was impossible for him, consistently with the plan of a progressive revelation, to make known always all the reasons of his procedure. Even with the clearer and fuller discoveries of the later revelation, as a key to the earlier, we may be sometimes unable to ascertain these reasons now. In contemplating some of those sterner aspects of the character of God which the earlier revelation exhibits, or those rigorous severities in his providence which it narrates, we may be apt to wonder if this is the same being whose love shines so conspicuously in the face of Jesus Christ. But when we candidly consider the nature of the case, compelling, if I may so speak, this glorious being, for a long season, to hide himself and his doings behind a cloud only partially dispelled, we see that we may well be expected to acquiesce in explanations not at all points free from doubt;—and for the rest be silent. Nay, more, we begin to suspect that we may perhaps err seriously, if we dwell only on what appears to be the milder view of the great Father presented to us in his Son, and to ask if, before all is over, and this very dispensation of grace has run its course, there may not be things seen and done on the earth that will but too terribly identify him whom men will persist in misrepresenting as the vengeful God of the Old Testament with him whom, to their cost, they may find that they have been equally misrepresenting as the all-indulgent and all-merciful God of the New.

II. It was the design of God that the revelation of his will to man should be, not theoretical and ideal, but practical, and, as it were, business-like, arising out of the circumstances, and adapted to the events and exigencies, of human history and human life. Whatever God revealed at any time of his mind and will, he revealed, as we say, *pro re nata*, for the occasion. What was revealed, therefore, took to a considerable extent, more or less, the form and mould of the occasion.

Even apart from this consideration, independently of

the occasion, the agency employed, being human agency, necessarily affects the substance as well as the form and manner of the revelation.

I suppose that truth, absolutely pure and perfect, can dwell only in the divine mind. To lodge it in the mind of a creature, exactly as it is in the mind of the Creator, may very probably be an impossibility.

It is said, indeed, that in the future state, "we shall know even as we are known." That, however, may not literally mean that our human knowledge is then to be completely assimilated to the divine knowledge, and made absolutely equal to it. It is rather intended to mark strongly the contrast, in this respect, between that future state and the present, in which "we know in part, and prophesy in part." In this life at all events, as is clear from that statement of the apostle, revelation, even when fullest and clearest, does not transfer truth identical and entire from the divine mind to the human; it does not give perfect, but only partial knowledge.

Now it is a true maxim of the schools, that "whatever is received, is received according to the capacity of the receiver." This maxim applies to a divine communication as well as to other things. Hence it may be freely admitted that gospel truth—the truth as it is in Jesus—even when communicated directly and immediately—to the inspired apostles for instance—was not to them, absolutely and perfectly, what it is to God. Even they "knew in part, and they prophesied in part."

Nay, more: it may be granted that it was not to any one of them exactly what it was to any other of them;

that no two of them saw it in exactly the same light themselves, or could present it in exactly the same light to others.

They were men of like passions with ourselves. They had their several idiosyncrasies; their individual peculiarities of thought and feeling; their distinctive temperaments and tastes. He must be either very blind or very bigoted, who refuses to admit that Paul, and James, and Peter, and John, had each his own conception of the revealed way of life and duty; and that, in writing their apostolic letters, they taught it each according to his own conception of it. Had it been otherwise, the New Testament would have been a very dull book; and what is worse, the mind of God would have been far less fully and adequately conveyed to us than as we have it now; unless, indeed, the writers were to be mere machines. It is the fact of our having the truth of the gospel presented to us by different men, looking at it from different standpoints, and conceiving of it somewhat differently from one another that enables us to obtain something better, at anyrate, than a merely one-sided view of that great mystery of godliness, which yet, after all, until our earthly house of this tabernacle is dissolved, we can know only in part.

But now, admitting and thankfully rejoicing in this fact, I urge it as what to my mind is one of the strongest of all arguments for the full and infallible inspiration of the apostolic writings. I cannot bring myself to believe that when God meant to reveal his will to me, to you, to all, in a matter, not of life and death merely, but of life and death for eternity; when he was about to communicate, as from himself, and on his own authority, the knowledge of the one only way of salvation; and when, for that purpose, he engaged the minds and pens of men, who, being men, could at the very best know it themselves only in part;—and who, moreover, being men of different habits and dispositions, could not but view it and present it differently from one another—I say I cannot bring myself to believe that he left these men to write without a superintendence and unerring oversight that would secure the literal and verbal accuracy of every sentence they composed; its being literally and verbally what he would have it to be; literally and verbally correct and true. I will not do my God so great wrong as to imagine that he could so act. I may have to admit that there are difficulties in connection with these precious remains, which I have not, in this remote age and country, the means of solving. But I for one will be no maker of difficulties; no eager finder of them; nor will I make too much of them when they force themselves upon me. I will not refuse a probable, or even a possible, explanation of them, merely because it does not clear up all, and make all certain. And most assuredly, even in a desperate case, I shall consider it infinitely more probable that there is some mistake on my part, some error in my way of looking at the matter; that the puzzle I am in is owing to my distance from the writers; that a few simple words from them would at once remove it;—and will remove it when I meet them in a better world;—than that either they should have undertaken, or God should have permitted them, to handle, as his authorised ambassadors, and the authoritative teachers of his Church in all ages, the deep things of his righteousness and peace, in any other words than those which his own Holy Spirit sanctioned and approved.

Returning now to the point on hand, I observe that not only must we take into account the human agency employed, as modifying the revelation of which the Bible is the record, but we must allow also for the human occasions to which it was adapted. Divine truth, as taught in Scripture, resembles mixed, rather than pure, mathematics. It is not like the abstract science of number or extension, but rather like the science of number or extension practically applied, in the mechanical arts, or in the transactions of business. In the Bible we have not merely God speaking from heaven, and man listening on earth; we have God, as it were, coming down to the earth, mixing himself up with its affairs, taking part in the ordinary ongoings of the world's history, turning the sayings and doings of men to account for the purpose of conveying the instruction which he wishes to impart.

Hence there is need of continual discrimination, that we may ascertain the true value and bearing of Scriptural statements as expressive of the divine mind and will.

With ordinary candour, the task of exercising the necessary discrimination is not really difficult. But it is easy, if one is so inclined, to create embarrassment; to confound the earthly occasion with the heavenly lesson; and to take exception to some things in the divine procedure which may appear to be inconsistent with the highest ideal of pure truth and perfect holiness, when in all fairness allowance ought to be made for the constraining force of circumstances. We must regard God, in those dealings of his with men which Scripture records, as in some sense laid under a restraint. It is no part of his purpose to coerce the human will, or to disturb and disarrange the ordinary laws which regulate the incidents of human life, and the progress of human society. There must be, on his part, a certain measure of accommodation. He cannot in his Word, any more than in his providence, have things precisely such, and so put, as the standard of absolute perfection would require. In legislating, for instance, for ancient Israel, it was not possible to have the ordinance of marriage, the usages of war, the rights of captives, the relation of master and servant,—and other similar matters affecting domestic order and the public weal,—regulated exactly as absolutely strict principle demands.

If it had been the plan of God to reveal his will by infallibly directing Plato in the framing of his idea of a perfect republic,—or our own Philip Sidney in composing his "Arcadia,"—there would have been none of the apparent anomalies which it delights the sceptic to detect, and which it sometimes vexes the devout reader to find, in the Mosaic writings, and in the books of Kings.

Even when the New Testament revelation was given, some things which it might have been expected that our Lord and his apostles would have regulated according to the perfect law of liberty, were left, as it would seem, undetermined. Evils were to be allowed to work themselves out, as it were, gradually in the course of time, through the growing Christian enlightenment of mankind; and the spirit of the gospel, as its influence was to be felt from age to age in every department of human experience, was naturally and spontaneously to effect salutary and blessed reforms, which it would have frustrated the very purpose for which the gospel was given to enact by formal statute, or enjoin in positive command. The disappearance of polygamy—the elevation of the female sex—the abolition of personal slavery in European Christendom—and other similar improvements in modern society, are instances in point.

In short, as regards both the teaching of truth and the enforcing of duty, the principle on which divine revelation has been given, "at sundry times and in divers manners," is very much the principle on which the Great Teacher himself acted in his personal ministry, when "he spake to the people in parables as they were able to bear it." And it is upon that principle, therefore, that the record of the revelation ought in all fairness to be interpreted and criticised.

If this common justice is done to it, not a few of the objections urged in certain quarters against its infallibility will be found to be altogether groundless. Nay, more, I am persuaded that if due regard be had to the consideration now stated, the presumption in favour of the infallibility of Scripture will appear to be very strong. I cannot see how otherwise we have any guarantee for the accuracy of a revelation, depending for the right understanding of it on a knowledge of the circumstances in which its separate and successive portions were communicated, unless we have these circumstances reported to us under an unerring oversight. And, I have no doubt that, were a comprehensive survey taken of all the various intimations of the mind of God contained in Scripture, viewed in the light of the historical and circumstantial occasions by which they were suggested, and to which they were accommodated, a singularly cogent, cumulative body of proof might be built up. It is, in fact, impossible to account for the wonderful harmony and consistency pervading the whole of the divine volume,—as the record of a revelation of God, growing out of, and growing into, the progress of the race of man,—on any other supposition than that the Spirit of God has so superintended the entire book throughout, as to insure, from the highest discoveries of heaven in it, down to the meanest details of earth, the infallible correctness of all its contents.

III. Revelation was to be natural and free, not stiff and formal. Those by whom it was to be given were to speak and write freely. It seems somehow to be imagined by some that men infallibly directed by the Holy Spirit, and conscious or assured of their being so, must feel themselves under the pressure of a strong restraint, obliged to pick their steps, if I may so say, with extreme nicety and delicacy; to be very scrupulous and fastidious in telling what they have to tell; carrying their anxiety about the rigid accuracy of everything they say to a pitch of punctiliousness that, in an ordinary speaker or writer, would be held to be either mere affectation, or ridiculous precision and pedantry. I apprehend that we might expect the very opposite effect to be produced on their modes of thought and expression. I can see no reason why the Holy Spirit, if he has any communication to make, should not use the same latitude that the most truthful of mankind allows himself to use, when minute exactness is not necessary, and is not pretended; as, for instance, when he thinks it quite enough to state a sum of years, or of people, in round numbers; or when he reports the speech of a friend, or of an orator, whose precise words he does not profess to give. Nay more, I can well believe that a man writing under the assurance of divine guidance, might be even less careful in matters of that sort than he would otherwise consider himself obliged to be; and might take liberties in dealing with certain subjects, which, if left to himself, he would by no means have considered it warrantable to take.

Let me illustrate what I mean by a very simple example, in a very trifling matter;—and then endeavour to show how the idea or principle which I have indicated may be applied to things of greater consequence.

I find Paul, in his First Epistle to the Corinthians, in his anxiety to meet the subdivisions among them—their taking sides, "I am of Paul, and I of Apollos, and I of Cephas, and I of Christ"—asking, with some indignation, "Is Christ divided? Was Paul crucified for you? Or were ye baptized in the name of Paul?" And then he adds, in his eager and anxious haste to disclaim his having ever given them any occasion for imagining that they should attach themselves to him, as if he had baptized them in his own name,—that he had not been in the practice of ordinarily baptizing them at all, and that it was now matter to him of high satisfaction that he had not: "I thank God that I baptized none of you, but Crispus and Gaius; lest any should say that I baptized in mine own name." Now this was a mistake; and I can fancy the amanuensis or scribe who wrote to Paul's dictation, stopping short to tell him so, and to refresh his memory; or else Paul recollects himself; for he goes on to say: "And I baptized also the house of Stephanas." Then, as if he felt that there might still be some omission, but that it was unnecessary to be more particular and precise, he adds: "Besides, I know not whether I baptized any other. For Christ sent me, not to baptize, but to preach the gospel." I give this as a slight illustration of the freedom with which an inspired apostle might write; that freedom being all the greater, in consequence of his being quite sure that in some way or other the accuracy of what he wrote would be sufficiently secured by the Divine Spirit, under whose infallible superintendence he knew himself to be writing.

Now, the consideration thus suggested may go far to explain not a few things that have been regarded as difficulties and objections in the way of the infallibility of Scripture. I shall mention only two. The one is,—the variations in the evangelical narratives; the other is,—the manner in which the Old Testament is quoted and referred to in the New.

1. As to the first, let me make a supposition.[1] Our blessed Lord, during his lifetime, or after his resurrection and before he went to heaven, might have desired four of his followers, who had been always with him in his ministry, to write down, separately and independently, what they could remember, and what they considered most worthy of being remembered, of his sayings and doings; and then to bring their several narratives to him, that he might revise and correct them. The knowledge that what they wrote was to be submitted to their Master's eye, would be a stimulus to all of them to do their best. But would it not also give them great boldness and freedom in executing their task? They would not feel themselves hampered by the constant fear of not giving *verbatim* every sentence of a discourse, and not stating every minute particular about a miracle; nor would they be haunted by the apprehension that their failing to do so might give rise to apparent discrepancies in their biographies. They would have little scruple in following very much each the bent of his own mind, as to the selection of materials, the order of their arrangement, and the language employed in recording them. There would be a free play and exercise of their faculties and feelings. Theirs would be the "pens of ready writers."

And now, they put their manuscripts into their Master's hands. What will be his treatment of them?

Will he insist on reducing them to a tame uniformity?

---

[1] This is partly a repetition of an illustration used in the former Lecture, only somewhat differently applied. I retain it for the sake of the completeness of this Lecture, as well as on account of the importance of the point at issue.

Will he be for retrenching here, enlarging there; over-crowding the canvas with details in one place; cutting out graphic incidents, graphically told, in another; altering and amending words and phrases, until the agreement becomes so close and complete as to defy the most captious fault-finder? Surely not. He will not thus give the appearance of collusion to what he designs to be distinct and independent testimonies. He will leave the memoirs in the freedom and freshness of their original spontaneous simplicity; only taking care that there is nothing in them for which he would not be willing himself to stand voucher. He prefers their easy and artless reminiscences to an absolutely perfect history, as giving really a truer and more life-like representation of himself. He suffers them to go forth under his sanction, although he quite well foresees that the different ways in which they tell the story of his life may give rise to questions that could only be solved by a fuller and more exact narrative than any one of all the four professes to be.

Now the case, thus put as a supposition, is virtually the case as in point of fact it actually is. Historians and biographers, enjoying the infallible guidance of the Divine Spirit, and knowing that they enjoyed it, would be sure to write in the free and natural way which I have described. The Spirit acting, if I may so speak, in the interest of Christ, and consulting for his glory, would exercise his superintendence, just as I have imagined Christ himself to conduct his revision. And the result, as might easily be shown in detail, would be the very *phenomena* which the Scriptural narratives, as we now have them, present.

2. The manner in which the Old Testament is quoted and referred to in the New, may also be explained, I think, at least partly, upon the same principle. This is a wide subject—far too wide to be discussed fully in this form. A very few hints regarding it must suffice for the present.

My notion is, that the apostles and evangelists may have been led to use more freedom than they would otherwise have ventured to use, in dealing with the Old Testament Scriptures, and connecting them with the New Dispensation, by the very fact of their being under infallible guidance. Nor is it difficult to see a good reason for this. The whole of the Old Testament has a prospective reference to the gospel. Its historical details, its typical institutions, its devotional pieces, its maxims of wisdom, its prophetic intimations—all point to Christ and the kingdom of Christ. Of necessity, however, all these foreshadowings of more substantial good things to come, are expressed in language less clear than what might and would naturally be employed when the good things had actually come. And let it be borne in mind, that the New Testament writers, when they quote or refer to the language of the Old, are not merely citing it in proof of what they teach. They are authoritatively interpreting it and applying it; drawing out its full meaning as it is developed by the later revelation. In these circumstances, their very consciousness, or assurance, of an infallible divine superintendence being exerted over them, might make them feel that they were warranted in exercising a large measure of discretion. Being under such a superintendence, they are not, like ordinary teachers, subject to the Scriptures which they handle. In an important sense they are masters of them : entitled to put their own sense and meaning on the statements and contents of these Scriptures; and entitled consequently, in large measure, to take their own way of making that sense and meaning clear.

When, therefore, a passage of Old Testament Scripture assumes in their hands a different import and bearing from what, as it stands in its original place, it seems to have, the presumption is, that the apparent difference arises from the limit which, by the very necessity of the case, was put upon the clearness of Old Testament discoveries;—that the apostle understands the prophet better than the prophet could understand himself, and expresses the meaning of the passage better than the prophet himself, in the circumstances, could express it. The same consideration may account generally for the free manner in which the authors of the New Testament cite the words of the Old. They do not study always literal and verbal accuracy. They interpret while they quote. They have respect to the use and application which they are making of the words, rather than to the mere words themselves; giving the true evangelical sense, if not the very terms in which originally that sense may have been more or less imperfectly conveyed.

All this seems to be capable of a reasonable and satisfactory explanation, on the supposition of an infallible divine guidance being incessantly exercised over what the apostles and evangelists wrote. I confess, however, that on any other supposition I consider it to be inexplicable. I can scarcely reconcile it, I would almost say, with fair dealing. At all events, I cannot reconcile it with that reverence for the very letter of their sacred books which was a peculiar characteristic of Jewish writers of old, and that sense of responsibility for even verbal correctness which men in their position must have owned. I am persuaded that the New Testament teachers felt themselves at liberty to deal with the Old Testament as freely as they did, solely because they were,—and because they knew that they were,—under the control and superintendence of the Spirit of Truth, who would not suffer them to err.

There are other circumstances connected with the use of the Old Testament in the New, which must be taken into account, if we would do full justice to the argument. I allude to certain Oriental and Jewish modes of thought and ways of looking at things, which differ much from the mental habits of Western and modern nations. They were not so analytical and discriminating as we are; not by any means so abstract; but rather prone to view objects in the concrete, and to group together as one person or thing what, when closely examined, may be found to resolve itself into several. But this, and other considerations bearing on the present topic, I must pass over.

IV. The fourth condition under which I assumed at the outset the divine revelation to be given, and the record of it to be framed, is, that the revelation was to be limited and restricted; not ranging over the whole field of possible knowledge in science or in history; but embracing only what concerns the moral government of God and the salvation of men.

Here, it is important to understand what the problem is which occasions difficulty.

What is it that the Divine Being, according to the plan which he proposes to himself, has, I ask with reverence, to do? He intends to reveal his will, not in an abstract form of ideal heavenly perfection, but in connection with earth's changes and the affairs of men. Of necessity, therefore, the revelation must not only touch the confines, but enter and occupy the domains, of scientific truth and secular history. But God did not mean to make either those whom he employed as his agents in giving the revelation, or the people to whom they gave it, wiser or better informed on these subjects, than they would have been without a revelation—except only in so far as it might be necessary for spiritual and moral ends. Hence, when the facts of science or of history come up, as it were, in the course of the giving of the revelation, and are to be dealt with or referred to,—this must be done in such a way as, on the one hand, not to anticipate the discoveries, or supersede the researches, which from age to age men are to make and institute for themselves, in the exercise of their natural faculties; and yet, on the other hand, not to be inconsistent with them. Very plainly this is a problem which the Divine Mind alone can meet and grapple with. To say nothing that shall tell men what God means that they should find out for themselves; and yet, to say nothing that shall be at variance with what they do ultimately find out for themselves; who can reconcile these opposite terms of this condition under which revelation is to be given, but God only?

And how, let me ask, may it be expected that the reconciliation shall become clear and certain to men?

At first, of course, there is no difficulty. The revelation is given, and the record of it is written, in accordance with the amount of information and the state of opinion at the time. The inspired Word is abreast of the science and literature of the age, but not in advance of it. By and by, the progress of inquiry brings out new information, and gives rise to new opinions, on those subjects which men have been left to investigate for themselves. The new information, and the new opinions, clash and come into collision with the method of interpreting Scripture hitherto in use, and the current notions which it has been supposed to sanction. Alarm is felt, as if the very foundations of revealed truth were shaken. The sun must move round the earth. Galileo dies, asserting, with his latest breath, that it is the earth that moves round the sun. "It moves! it moves!" cries the martyr in the cause of science;—a martyr also, as it turns out, in the cause of revelation too.

This is the second stage in the advance of man towards the right apprehension of the plan and method of the revelation of God. It is a natural and inevitable stage. And we are not to judge too severely, either on the one hand the students of nature, who may have been tempted, in this stage, to raise reluctant doubts as to the scientific accuracy of revelation; or on the other hand the students of revelation, who may have been led by these doubts being raised to show an unworthy jealousy and fear of the free study of nature.

But a better understanding comes. It is found, on closer study, that while the Bible does not teach the new doctrines of science, which it could not do consistently with its general design, yet it does not teach the opposite, or the reverse of them. And that is all that can be reasonably asked. Not only so. When that is made clear, it furnishes a most striking and irrefragable proof of the infallibility of the Bible; its having been composed under the eye and hand of an infallible Mind, knowing all things from the beginning, and taking care that whatever of truth is revealed and written down, from time to time, partially and incompletely, to meet the successive exigencies of human sin, and suffering, and sorrow, and salvation, shall be, on the one hand, adapted to the existing state of knowledge at the time; and, on the other hand, consistent with all that ever can be known. The Bible has hitherto stood this test. The Bible alone can stand it. All other pretended revelations teach, as an essential part of themselves, positively false cosmogonies, false deluges, impossible miracles. In contrast, the Bible stands alone.

I may be allowed here to refer to a remark made some years ago in conversation by the lamented Hugh Miller, which at the time impressed me much, and which I have never forgotten. It was to this effect. The geological discoveries as to the earth's existence and history before the Adamic creation are consistent with a probable, or possible, interpretation of Genesis: not indeed with any interpretation that would naturally have occurred to any reader before these discoveries were made—that would have been to forestall the discoveries by revelation; but still with an interpretation of which the inspired words are fairly susceptible. The Confession and Catechisms of the Westminster divines, on the other hand, in treating of the subject of the creation, use language that cannot in any way be harmonised with the teachings of science. Of course this is not wonderful. These learned men, being uninspired, could not make provision for a state of knowledge not yet reached. They gave their judgment on questions actually before them, and cannot be considered authoritative on a point which was not then raised. But the argument which the contrast between them and the sacred writer suggests is very striking. There is reserve on the part of Moses. The inspiring and superintending Spirit does not give him scientific information in advance of his age. But care is taken that, writing according to the scientific views of his age, he shall say nothing that is to be found ultimately incompatible or irreconcilable—in the judgment of any candid mind, duly considering the conditions of the problem—with what the advancing march of inquiry is to go on unfolding to the end of time.

I have done, as I best could, what I proposed to do. I have not only not exhausted the subject; I have scarcely even touched its arguments. I have endeavoured simply to state the question; to lay down the conditions under which it might be assumed beforehand, that the Bible, as the infallible record of an infallible revelation, would be written; and to suggest some of the features which the Bible, written under these conditions, might be expected to exhibit.

Suffer one closing word. There is a very vulgar outcry in certain learned quarters against bibliolatry. Some of our learned Grecians positively cannot keep their temper, when they have to speak of a believer in an infallible Bible. And lesser scholars chime in. For it looks like manliness to put an infallible Bible in the same category with an infallible Church or an infallible Pope—to turn the tables upon biblical Protestants, and taunt them with their submission to an infallible Book, as if that were equivalent to their kissing the toe of an infallible priest.

With all deference to our iconoclastic friends, there is some little difference between these two attitudes.

To stand erect in the presence of my God and Father in heaven, and with his Book in my hand and in my heart —the Book which he has caused to be written, and written infallibly, for my learning—to confer and commune directly with himself about its contents, asking him to open it up to me, and to open my eyes that I may behold wonders out of it; and, on the faith of the wonders I behold in it, to pour forth my inmost soul before him, unbosoming all my grief, confessing all my sin, accepting all his mercy;—alone—myself alone with him alone;—to settle and seal, upon this authentic record of his will, a holy covenant of peace;—who dare say—what Grecian pedant, what shallow sceptic—that a transaction like that on my part with my God—so close, so direct, so personal, so confidential—proceeding all throughout on his speaking to me in this infallible Bible, and my speaking to him in reliance on its infallibility,—has anything at all in common with the blind, implicit trust which allows a man—a mere man, though he be clothed in scarlet, and wear a triple crown, and have the backing of solemn conclaves and councils—to set the Book aside;—and himself come in between me and the God of my salvation, asking me to receive the law at his mouth, and let him negotiate for me the relation in which I am to stand to Heaven? If I can dispense with guidance out of myself altogether—if, while willing to receive hints from all quarters, I am prepared to say that I need not, and that I will not, take authoritative instructions from any—then away equally with an infallible Bible and an infallible Pope. But, if conscious of my own ignorance and insufficiency, my guilt and misery, I long for good news from heaven to meet my case, shall I take the good news at second-hand from the mouth of a poor mortal like myself? Or shall I thankfully welcome, embrace, study, meditate on, and pray over the Book, the blessed Book, in which my heavenly Father himself has taken care to have the message of his grace in his Son unerringly recorded,—the Book which he has also promised, by his Holy Spirit, to open up to me sufficiently for my everlasting salvation, to his own eternal glory?

CONSCIENCE AND THE BIBLE.

CONSCIENCE AND THE BIBLE.

CONSCIENCE and the Bible have a common meeting-point behind, as it were, or above,—in law; and a common meeting-place in front,—in virtue. As they point upwards or backwards, their lines meet in divine law; as they tend forwards or downwards, their lines meet in human virtue.

This thought might be presented in a sort of diagram. Look at an elongated diamond-shaped figure. At the extremities of a line drawn across between the two larger angles, let conscience and the Bible stand inscribed; conscience on the left, the Bible on the right. The other two extremities, those of a line joining the smaller angles, may indicate the relative positions, the one of law, the other of virtue. Beginning at a point marked for law, draw two diverging lines till they reach two other points, opposite to one another, marked for conscience and the Bible respectively; thereafter let the lines converge till they come together in a fourth point; that point may be marked as denoting virtue.

Such is a sort of geometrical representation of the positions occupied by law, the Bible, conscience, virtue, relatively to one another. Law is prior to both conscience and the Bible; it is recognised as prior by both of them; both of them look up to it and do it homage. Virtue again is under them; it appeals to them; they judge it. Conscience and the Bible acknowledge law; they approve virtue. And across the line joining law and virtue, conscience and the Bible meet.

What then is law, as acknowledged by conscience and the Bible? What is the virtue which they approve? These are the two questions on the answer to which the solution of a third question, as to the mutual relations of the two authorities,—conscience and the Bible,—may largely depend.

I. What is law, as acknowledged by conscience and the Bible? It is a moral law; a law of right and wrong. But of what nature?

It is, perhaps, unfortunate that the word law is ambiguous. It has one meaning when it is used as a term of jurisprudence, and another meaning altogether when it is applied to the phenomena of natural science. What is called the law of the land, for instance, is felt by all men to be a thing quite distinct, generically, from the physical laws, or the laws of instinct. These last are generalizations of facts observed; the other is a rule authoritatively promulgated and judicially enforced. The result of a fair induction of particular instances is embodied and expressed in a general formula, to which we give the name of law. It is a natural law, or a law of nature, thus ascertained, that bodies gravitate towards one another, and that the force of gravitation is inversely as the square of the distance. To most minds this language conveys a very different idea from what they receive, when they are told that the laws under which they live as citizens forbid and punish crime.

That the divine law is essentially the same in principle with human law, both conscience and the Bible clearly teach. The obligation to obey the law of God, commends itself to conscience as identically of the same kind with the obligation to obey the law of the land. And in the Bible, the magistrate is represented as wielding an authority of the same kind with the authority of Deity. The rulers of the people are called gods.

The mere mention of this distinction must be enough. But as it touches a point of supreme importance, and as a view adverse to that now stated is widely prevalent in influential quarters, it is necessary to go into the subject more fully.

The order established in creation is one of the surest evidences of a creative mind. The more thoroughly it is observed, tested, ascertained and developed, by the inquiries of science, the more conclusively is it seen and felt to be so. Ranging over the myriads of ages of which our globe retains the traces; subjecting the multitudinous stars of heaven to her far-seeing telescope, and the all but prophetic calculations of her exact mathematics; embracing all the living tribes that have ever peopled the earth; mastering all the relations of social life, and all the conditions of social prosperity;—science seeks to reduce the whole complex mechanism and manifold movements of the universe to a sort of uniformity, if not to unity. And the more successful she is in this, the more thoroughly does she establish the reign of one infinite and omnipotent Intelligence, planning all, and presiding over all.

Now, law is the index, the assertor, the vindicator of order. If there is to be order, there must be law. And it must be law with its appropriate penalty. The more simple and universal the law—the more self-acting and self-enforcing—the more perfect the order. Hence the tendency, in the various departments of physical knowledge, to resolve particular inductions into more comprehensive general maxims—to trace a similarity of proportion throughout them all—to find the principles of sound, of colour, of form, of weight and motion, identical; so that music, painting, architecture, and the kindred arts, are said to be based on similar ratios or relations of number; and such powers as those of light, heat, electricity, galvanism, gravitation, converge towards some one radical element in the constitution of matter, that is to cover the phenomena of them all. Even apart from these higher speculations, the sense of law, as the security of order, which is originally strong in the human mind, gains additional strength through the investigation of nature. All things proceed according to law; and law implies intelligence and design.

It seems but another step in the same direction, to reduce the moral world also under the same rigid uniformity of rule and order with the physical. There, too, the empire of law reigns. There are laws according to which our intellectual, our active, our social, and our moral faculties are respectively regulated in their exercise.

There are laws of association governing the intellect; laws of motive and habit guiding the active powers; laws of taste and feeling controlling the social propensities; and laws of truth, righteousness, and love, determining the moral judgments. Thus man, as to his whole nature, is the subject of law. He thinks and acts, he likes or dislikes, he approves or condemns, according to law—according to laws proper to the different departments of his complex constitution. The violation of any of these laws is his misfortune, or fault,—and his misery. It is so, whichever of them it may be that is violated. The disorder, the evil, may be greater, when it is the law of a higher department of his nature, than when it is the law of a lower one. Redress and reparation may be more difficult. But it is an injury of the same kind that is done in both cases; it is a law of the same kind that is broken.

The apparent symmetry of a system like this has an attraction for minds of a certain order. But how does it stand the test of an appeal to consciousness? Try it in a single instance.

I dash my foot against a stone. A physical law is outraged by me. It vindicates itself: I suffer. But look at the different circumstances in which this may happen. It is a mere accident—I am pitied. It is the result of gross carelessness—I am pitied and laughed at. It is an injury inflicted on me—I am pitied, and a desire is felt to avenge me of my adversary. It is, on my part, a deliberate attempt to put an obstacle in the way of a crowded train—I am execrated as a monster. It is a prompt impulse, at the risk of life, to take an obstacle out of its way—I am lauded to the skies for my benevolence and bravery.

Here there are several distinct laws—call them laws of nature if you will—under which the same act or event is considered, tried, and judged. It is not with the same sentiment,—it is not even with similar sentiments,—that the violation or observance of these several laws is regarded. The violation or observance of the physical law which regulates the contact of two hard bodies, as of my foot and a stone, cannot be reduced to the same category with the violation or observance of the law which injustice and wanton cruelty are felt to break, and which courage in a good cause fulfils and honours. No sophistry can identify things which differ so widely. The instinct of mankind revolts against the attempt.

Let it be granted that God governs by law all his creatures, from dead and shapeless matter, up through all the gradations and developments of organization and life, to the highest order of mind. Is it law of the same kind throughout? Does not mind, intelligent and free, as it is found in man, come in contact with a law wholly unlike what holds dominion in the region of matter,—and in the region of mind, as it unfolds itself among the most sagacious of the other living racés around us?

Some points of contrast may be noted between this higher law and all the other laws of nature and being.

In the first place, these other laws are, all of them, as we apprehend them, the products of induction. That higher law we have by pure and simple intuition. That there are certain fixed and general laws to which the processes of nature and the energies of life in the universe are amenable, we learn—and what they are we learn—*a posteriori*, by observation and experience—the observation and experience of ourselves and others. The study of these laws is an inductive study. The sciences which treat of them are inductive sciences. It is true, that we can and do bring to bear upon them the intuitions of mathematics,—the *a priori* laws of thought which give us the necessary conditions of time and space. It is under these conditions that we investigate the phenomena of creation, and systematize or codify its laws. Still, essentially, they are laws forced upon us, *a posteriori*, by induction. The moral law is impressed upon us, *a priori*, by intuition. That there is a law of right and wrong, we know—and what it is, we know—by an original and primary intuition. It is a law of thought, exactly as those laws are, out of which geometry and algebra are evolved. The study of it is a deductive study. The science of ethics is a deductive science. It is true, that as we have to apply this law to the phenomena of voluntary action, there is occasion for observation and experience; and the more there is of a large and wise induction the better. In that view, the science which deals with this law is a mixed science. It is like the science which applies the axioms and demonstrations of the pure mathematics to the phenomena of practical astronomy. Still, the law itself is not one which we arrive at through any process of induction. It is known by intuition. It is given as an *a priori* law of thought —an original principle of moral judgment.

In the second place, this law is necessary, universal, eternal. These others are contingent. There is no absolute necessity, in the nature of things, for their being always and everywhere the same. We can conceive of a world in which the law of gravitation might be different from what it is here. The idea is not felt to involve a contradiction in terms, or an impossibility in thought. But we cannot even imagine the possibility of an alteration of the law of right and wrong. We can no more conceive of its being right to commit murder, and wrong to love our neighbour, than we can conceive of two and two being five and not four.

It is easy, indeed, to make difficulties about this, as sceptical writers have often done. Look, they say, at the varieties of opinion among nations—some justifying and commending as virtues what others condemn as crimes: Sparta encouraging cleverness and success in theft; the Hindoos admiring the conjugal devotion of the widow, as she casts herself on her husband's funeral pile, and commending the maternal piety which sends the tender babe away from the pollutions and ills of life, at once, through the holy river, into a better land. In all such instances as these, however, the bare statement of them, if it be a fair statement, shows that what really is commended is some quality universally felt and allowed to be commendable. The ill-informed and ill-regulated mind, misled by a partial or erroneous induction, comes exclusively to dwell on that quality,—to the omission of other features of the transaction which impart to it an entirely opposite character. There is nothing, therefore, in these instances that militates against the truth, which consciousness attests, that the law of right and wrong is not contingent,—that it is not arbitrary or discretionary, like those other laws of nature which, for anything we can see, might have been, and may yet be, different from what they are,—but that it is necessary and universal, like the axioms of intuitive science. In other words, the law of God is, like God himself, eternal and immutable.

But thirdly, and chiefly, this law has in it an element which none of these other laws, not even the laws of number and extension, possess,—the element of command. It speaks as having authority. It says, Thou shalt, and thou shalt not. It makes me say, I ought, and I ought not.

The physical law of heat tells me a fact, that fire burns; and it suggests an inference, that if I go into yonder burning fiery furnace, I shall be consumed and perish. It does not certainly say, Thou shalt go; neither, however, does it say, Thou shalt not go. And if the alternative be between that and worshipping the golden image, there is a law which says, imperatively, Thou shalt go; for it says, Thou shalt worship the Lord alone, and him only shalt thou serve.

The physical law of health tells me a fact, that excessive toil and scanty food wear out the body; and it suggests the inference, that if I toil the livelong day and night, and give myself but a crust of bread to eat, I must ere long sink and die. It does not certainly say, Thou shalt thus work in thy want; neither, however, does it say, Thou shalt not. And if the alternative be between that and theft, there is a law which says, imperatively, Thou shalt; for it says imperatively, Thou shalt not steal.

Even when the physical law comes nearest the moral law, this distinction is to be observed. The physical law of health tells the young man a certain fact, that sinful indulgence breeds disease; and it suggests the salutary inference, that if he continues in the sin, he must expect to reap the fruit of it in loathsome agony. Even here, however, it is not that law which speaks with a voice of command, but the law which says, Thou shalt not commit adultery; Lust not in thy heart; Thou shalt not covet.

In the fourth place, it is a consequence of this element of rightful supremacy residing in the moral law, and distinguishing it from all the others, that the breaking of it is something radically and essentially distinct from the breaking of any of them.

A man might be so wrong-headed as to insist on working a question in arithmetic in defiance of the law of number, that two and two are four; or he might try to master a problem in geometry by going in the teeth of the law of extension, that two straight lines cannot enclose a space. Of course he makes a mess of his sum and his solution. It is an instance of mental aberration; the man is mad, we say; and that is all. A similar madness or wrong-headedness might lead some extravagant idealist, out-Berkeleying Berkeley, to act upon his theory of the non-existence of matter, so as to knock his head against every post,—coming into collision with all the material laws of force and weight.

But apart from extreme cases, what are the terms,

even the strongest terms, which we can fairly use in characterizing conduct that is opposed to what these natural laws would seem to recommend? It is ignorance, or inadvertence, or imprudence. The worst we can say of it is, that it is imprudence. And none of these terms are terms of reproach necessarily—not even imprudence. They are quite consistent with innocence, and indeed even with merit. A strong sense of duty, an impulse of patriotic or generous feeling, will be accepted, any day, by the people,—the best judges by far in such a matter, —as a set-off against the most flagrant disregard of all the ordinary considerations of caution and wisdom. And when either ignorance, or inadvertence, or imprudence is alleged as a moral imputation against any one who has acted otherwise than these natural laws, if they had been duly attended to, would have led him to act, and who has consequently brought misfortune on himself and others, it will invariably be found that the higher law comes in. Some precept or some principle of that law has been outraged. And the measure of reproach is not the violation, more or less wilful, of those natural laws, but the indifference, or the opposition, which the act in question involves, to the eternal law of rectitude and duty.

Then again, on the other hand, ignorance, inadvertence, imprudence,—any of these pleas,—may explain or palliate my conduct, viewed as in antagonism to the natural laws. But none of them, nor all of them, will meet the case when the moral law is concerned. I did it because I knew no better; I did it without consideration and by mistake; it was very senseless and unwise in me to do it;—so you say when you have gone against any of the laws which regulate the sequences of events,—their following one another according to a certain order in the physical, mental, and social world; so you say, and there is no more to be said. You take the consequence. Or, perhaps, by some happy chance, or some shrewd afterthought, or some wise appliance under a system that admits of remedies and compensations, you escape the consequence. At all events, learning by experience, you are more wary in time to come.

Look now at Saul of Tarsus, consenting to the death of Stephen. He does it ignorantly, not knowing what he does, thinking that he is doing God service. He does it inadvertently, not considering sufficiently what he is about. It is the height of imprudence; even with the light which he has he had better pause, according to the sagacious counsel of Gamaliel. A wiser and calmer man would not at that juncture commit himself against the Christians. Is that all? Does that exhaust the case? Then, what is the meaning of the keen remorse which seems always, in the midst of his happiest experience of mercy, to haunt the memory of Paul?—"For I am the least of the apostles, that am not meet to be called an apostle, because I persecuted the church of God" (1 Cor. xv. 9).

There is a law, the breach of which—whatever plea of ignorance, or inadvertence, or imprudence, may be urged—is a very different matter from the crossing or traversing of any of the instituted laws of nature. It is the eternal law, the transgression of which is SIN.

Hence, finally, in the fifth place, it would seem to follow that the manner in which offences against these other natural laws are dealt with, affords no safe analogy for judging of the procedure on the part of the lawgiver, which transgressions of this moral law may require.

Every law of nature is enforced, or enforces itself, by an appropriate penalty. The penalty is the destruction of whoever or whatever thwarts the law. It is a penalty sure and inevitable, unless means are found to make the person or thing offending conformable again to the law, and to prevent or repair the injury which his or its non-conformity might do to the system of which he or it is a part. It is a principle of the divine government, even in the lower spheres of material and sentient nature, that the evil resulting from a breach of any of its laws is either worked out of the system by the destruction of the peccant member, or is repaired by some process of amelioration and neutralization; amelioration as to the peccant member, and neutralization as to the tendency of what is peccant to grow and perpetuate itself.

I fall, and break my arm. I break a physical law, and the penalty is the destruction of the limb. But there is a provision of nature which not only knits the fractured bone, but compensates the system for any harm that the fracture might do to it. So I escape the penalty; I am safe in the use of my forfeited member still; and my body is all the stronger for the accident.

Upon this analogy, an attempt has been made, not wisely, as I think, nor successfully, to explain the manner in which, according to the Christian system, the great

Lawgiver deals with sin as the transgression of his law. That law is held to be of the very same nature with the other laws on which the order of creation seems to depend. And the wonderful provision made by God for meeting the case of man's violation of it, is represented as identical in principle with those remedial provisions which abound in nature, and by which injuries happening under the laws of nature are repaired and redressed,—with no ultimate damage, either to the member offending or to the system to which it belongs, but rather with benefit to both.

It would be unsuitable to enlarge on this topic here, and now. Let it suffice to say, that such a view is not more dangerous in its theological aspect than it is inadequate, at least, if not unsound, in its philosophy. It confounds things that differ. It makes no sufficient account of that moral government, that divine and eternal system of jurisprudence, which such ideas as those of authority, right, duty, obligation, responsibility, guilt, blame, crime—ideas expressed in every language, and, therefore, indicating a universal instinct or intuition of the human mind—prove to be the highest order in the universe. And surely we speculate somewhat too wildly when we aspire to master the policy of Heaven; as if we could grasp, in some principle or formula of unity that we think we have found out, the whole vast and complicated plan of the divine administration. It is more in accordance with the humility of true science, as well as with the humility which does not seek to be wise above what is written, to accept the facts of conscience and the statements of revelation on the particular subject in hand, —the transgression of the moral law,—in their plain meaning, instead of aiming at so wide a generalization. And if we do, we shall stand on surer ground. We receive the combined testimony of conscience and revelation as to the demerit of sin, the reality of judgment, the necessity of satisfaction. And we adore the righteousness and love of the mysterious propitiatory sacrifice of the cross.[1]

Such, then, is law, as acknowledged by conscience and the Bible; the law to which both do homage.

1. The homage which conscience does to it is the recognition of its legitimate authority. That faculty or principle of our moral nature asserts a right of supremacy over all the particular affections, whether of self-love or of social love, by which men are moved to action. It has paramount authority within the domain of voluntary choice. It is, however, a delegated authority, and it is felt to be so. In fact, its own authority lies in its apprehension of the authority of law. To assert and vindicate the authority of law is its proper function. It is only in so far as it is competent to the discharge of that function, that its own title to command is valid. Can, then, its competency be relied on?

To interpret and apply the law is an office requiring information. The bearing of the law on any particular case can be rightly determined only when the information respecting that case is exact and full. It is not the

[1] I refer here with regret, among other instances, to a recent work by the author of the "Philosophy of the Plan of Salvation."

province of conscience to collect information. It calls for information. It imposes the duty of inquiry. But the conduct of the inquiry is devolved on the ordinary powers of the understanding. These are liable to err through their own infirmity, or the absence of the means of knowledge. They may represent the case otherwise than it really is. The obligation of the law of right and wrong may, in consequence, be asserted erroneously. But, strictly speaking, that is not the fault of conscience.

Again, if the power whose function it is to vindicate the law is to discharge that function well, it must rule *de facto,* or in fact,—as well as *de jure,* or in right. A usurper, displacing it from its seat of authority, may succeed in silencing it; or he may impose upon it by false representations; or he may subject it to a torture that makes it incapable of true discernment. Such a usurper is the will—the masterful will—backed by his accomplice, habit. No faculty or affection in us, except the will, can set aside conscience. But the will can do it. And it can do it so perseveringly, and so violently; it can so imprison conscience in its own den, and so bandage the eyes through which conscience sees, that law—the law of right and wrong—shall be asserted very fitfully and very feebly, and shall soon cease to be asserted at all. But neither is this, strictly speaking, the fault of conscience.

Still, in so far as the understanding is fallible, and the will powerful, the competency, or at least the sufficiency of conscience, as the vindicator and assertor of law, is indirectly, if not directly, affected. And if the understanding is darkened, and the will debauched by sin, the risk of fraud or force interfering with its fair and free discharge of that function is immensely increased.

In itself, moreover, directly as well as indirectly, conscience is injured and defiled by the entrance into the human constitution of that blight of moral evil which has vitiated the whole nature of man. The very facility with which it accepts the representations of a darkened understanding, and yields to the force of a debauched will, proves it to be not only infirm and irresolute, but inclined towards the side which these other powers would have it to tolerate, if not to favour. It has lost that high tone of faithful and cordial loyalty to the law and the Lawgiver to which, were man in a right state, both the understanding and the will would be constrained to defer.

Nevertheless, as regards its capacity of recognising both the character and the authority of divine law, the conscience is upon the whole intact. The corruption of our nature has not so vitiated the conscience as to invalidate its conclusions when it discriminates between right and wrong, or deprive it of its right to rule and be obeyed. If it had, our guilt would have been less, and our recovery would have been impossible. For it is through the conscience alone that a fallen, but yet free, intelligence can be reached. It is to the conscience that the violated law appeals. It is the conscience that accepts the sentence of condemnation. It is the conscience that pleads guilty of sin as the transgression of the law, and welcomes the assurance of a sufficient expiation, and an adequate satisfaction. Liberated from the aberrations of an understanding darkened by alienation from God, and from the excesses of a will at enmity with God,—liberated from both of these extraneous influences—quickened, also, and purged, by the Spirit, through belief of the truth,—the conscience rejoices in its recovered power,—a power flowing from its own free and loving allegiance to the law, as the law of liberty and love,—to be the effectual as well as the legitimate vindicator of its authority.

There is another manner in which the conscience may be set free—free to see, to know, to assert, the whole melancholy and appalling truth—when the guilty come to be dealt with, not in mercy, but in judgment; when they stand to receive their sentence at the bar of God,—and pass away to endure it,—compelled, in their own despite, to own the righteousness and majesty of law.

Such is the homage which conscience does to the law.

2. As to the Bible, not to speak of the glorious eulogies, in either Testament, which extol and celebrate the excellency of the law of the Lord, nor of the deep emotions of reverence and delight with which holy men meditate on its perfection; let the view which the Bible gives, throughout all its revelations, of the actual present government under which the human race is placed, be well considered. It is impossible to find consistency in the sacred records on any other supposition than this—that mankind are living on the earth under a respite. The analogy of religion, natural and revealed, can be fully brought out only upon that hypothesis. Men, here and now, are spirits in prison. The whole human family is under sentence of condemnation. The sentence is suspended. For the race, it is suspended till what Scripture

calls the consummation of all things; for individual members of the race, it is suspended till the moment of death. It is, however, only suspended. And the condition on which it is suspended, the end for which it is suspended,—as well as the ultimate issues of the experiment in regard to those who do, and those who do not, acquiesce in the condition of its suspension, and reach the end which the suspension is designed to serve,—are all unfolded in the Bible. They are so unfolded, moreover, as to present and submit to the free choice of all men the one only alternative of which the case admits,—the alternative of prompt submission carrying with it an immediate, legal justification, or of prolonged lawlessness and rebellion, sealing the inevitable doom of legal condemnation. It is homage to law throughout.

On this subject it is relevant to quote, as summing up the argument, the closing paragraph of the "Examination of Maurice's Theological Essays" (p. 480), in which the controversy at issue between him and his examiner is reduced to a single question:—

"That question, as it seems to me, concerns the nature of the government of God. Is it a government of law? Does God rule intelligent beings by a law? Certainly, I may be told. Who doubts it? The government of God is a government of law,—of the law of love. But I must be allowed again to ask, In what sense is it a government of law? For the familiar use of the expression, 'laws of nature,' has introduced an ambiguity into this phrase. What is a government of law, a government by law? If I am absolutely dependent upon a being possessed of certain tastes, under the influence, let it be supposed, of a particular ruling passion,—if he and I are inseparably bound together, so that I must make up my mind to receive all my good from him, and find all my good in him, such as he is; then, in his tastes, in his ruling passion, I have a law, conformity to which is the condition of my wellbeing. Obviously, however, this ruling passion in him is a law to me, in precisely the same sense in which any quality in matter is a law to me; in that sense and in no other. My intimate connection with the material world makes conformity to the unchanging principles, according to which its movements proceed, a condition of my wellbeing as a creature endowed with a physical nature. My intimate connection with the being or person with whom I am living, and am always to live, makes conformity to the unchanging principles, or habit, or ruling passion according to which he uniformly feels and acts, the condition of my wellbeing as a being endowed with the capacity of feeling and acting as he does. Let his ruling passion be pure charity or love. Then, in one sense, there is a law of love brought into contact with my will. The law of love is unbending, and it has in it an element of wrath against the unlovely. My will is perverse, apt to incline towards subjection to a usurping tyrant or an intruding tempter, capable of almost infinite resistance. But the law of love works steadily on. It unfolds and reveals itself, it embodies itself in action, it is manifested wonderfully in a redeeming and regenerating economy, and ultimately one cannot see how it can fail to bring my will, and every reasonable will, into accordance with itself. For anything I can perceive, government by law in any other sense than this, is not recognized at all in the theology of these Essays. It is needless to add, that the whole theology of those who are commonly considered orthodox and evangelical divines, is based upon an entirely different conception both of government and of law. According to them it is an administrative government that God exercises,—a government embracing in it legislation, judicial procedure, calling to account, awarding sentences. It is an authoritative law, with distinct sanctions annexed to it, that God promulgates and enforces. This is what they understand when they speak of God being a moral Ruler as well as a holy and loving Father. They cannot rid themselves of the impression that both Scripture and conscience attest the reality of such a government and such a law. It is under that impression that they draw out from Scripture, to meet the anguish of conscience, those views of the guilt of sin and its complete expiation, the corruption of nature and its thorough renovation,—those views of pardon, peace, reconciliation, reward, which they delight to urge upon all men in the name of Him who "hath no pleasure in the death of the wicked, but that the wicked should turn unto him and live." And it is under the same impression that they think they find, in the essential freedom of the will of man as a responsible agent, an explanation, on the one hand, of the possibility of evil entering into the universe under the rule of a good and holy God; and on the other hand also, a probable explanation of the impossibility of there being any provision of mercy brought within the reach of men, which does not imply a provision also for the case of that mercy being neglected or refused."

II. Conscience and the Bible approve virtue as they acknowledge law. What is this virtue? And what is the approbation with which not only man, but God regards it?

The first of these questions it is not very important, either for philosophical or for practical purposes, to answer. What is virtue? Is there any common quality that characterizes and identifies all the actions or dispositions that are said to be virtuous? Yes, one may say; they are all useful; useful to the individual; useful to society. Utility is the test of virtue. It may be so. Perhaps this is the simplest and most obvious common quality that can be named. The habits and frames of mind that win approbation are such as are useful. What then? Is it for their utility that they are approved? The instinct of mankind says, No. As supplying an argument from final causes for the goodness of God, the fact that the things which we approve as virtuous are found invariably, on the whole, to be useful, may deserve notice. That is not, however, the element which constitutes their virtue, or, if the term may be allowed, their virtuousness. Nor is much gained when we add the element of intention or choice, and resolve all virtue into a desire to be useful, or into benevolence, or good-will, or any other single affection. The truth is, the affections which we approve as virtuous vary indefinitely in their nature, and in the circumstances in which they are exercised. No attempt to run them up into one common attribute has succeeded. To discriminate, describe, and classify them is all that can be done. That is the province of practical ethics.

The second inquiry, into the nature of the approbation with which virtue is regarded, or into the state of mind which it occasions in one contemplating it, is more interesting. Here, too, an extreme passion for simplicity is to be deprecated. What we call approbation, is a complex state of mind. It is not easy to give in short compass an exhaustive analysis of it. But if allowance be made for what, perhaps, may appear to some to be too fanciful a theory,—I think the harmony of conscience and the Bible on this subject may be placed in a somewhat striking and graphic light.

Take one of those states of mind which are admitted to possess a moral character, whether good or bad, and trace it in its effects upon the moral observer.

In the first place, the mere conception of it—the bare, naked apprehension of it in the mind—gives rise, instantaneously, to a double movement in the department with which it first comes in contact. That department comprehends the power or faculty of distinguishing what is true from what is false, as well as what is fair and beautiful from what is the reverse. These two functions, the judgment and the taste—the discernment of truth and the sense of beauty—are intimately connected, if, indeed, they are not all but identical. They are both of them immediate and instantaneous in their action, and they are mutually the handmaids of each other. A mathematical proposition or demonstration, seen to be true, is felt also to be beautiful. It appeals to the taste, as well as to the judgment; and in proportion as it satisfies and convinces the judgment, it pleases and gratifies the taste. We speak of a beautiful theorem, and it is the sense of beauty no less than the perception of truth, which, when the difficulty of the search is overcome, and the discovery successfully made, prompts the exclamation of delight, I have found it! I have found it! On the other hand, in the peculiar field of taste, if any object awaken the sense of beauty, it will be found, at the same time, to command the acquiescence of the judgment in it, as in what is true. When the eye rests on a fair form or a beauteous scene, not only is it agreeable and soothing to the taste, but the judgment also approves of it as consistent with the truth of things. When I am admiring a picture, or statue, or landscape, I am conscious of a calm conviction of reality, similar to what I experience when I assent to an abstract demonstration, just as, in return, when I perceive the conclusive certainty of an abstract demonstration, I feel a gratification of taste, precisely such as the visible comeliness of nature calls forth. Nor is this connection between the judgment and the taste altogether unaccountable. They are both simple acts or operations of the mind; and what is common to both is the apprehension of contrariety and disunion removed, and consistency, compactness, or, in a word, unity, established or restored.

In morals, this blending of the judgment and the taste is very discernible. Let an evil action or an evil state of mind be contemplated, and there is an uneasy apprehension of its opposition to truth, along with a painful and oppressive sense of its deformity and unloveliness. The judgment finds the true relations of things divided and dissevered, and the taste recoils from the dislocation. Let the opposite virtue be observed, and the faculty of comparison discerns agreement, coherence, union, in the fitness of things as now adjusted, while the sense of beauty rests and reposes in the harmony.

But there is a second and inner chamber into which these actions or states of mind, apprehended, in the first or outer chamber, as either true and beautiful, or false and foul, must now pass; and that chamber is the seat of the emotions. The transition here is from the head to the heart—from the mind, sitting in judgment at the gate, and looking out with quick eye for all that is grand or fair, to the bosom in whose depths the springs of feeling lie. Through the judgment and the taste, moral actions or states of mind reach and set in motion the affections; and, as in the department of simple apprehension,—the outer hall of the soul,—there is a double exercise of vigilance, and, as it were, a double scrutiny of all comers, so, in their reception within, there is a double movement or excitement among the dwellers there. The affections are doubly stirred. Are both of the watchers satisfied? Do both of them concur in warranting the entrant? Does the judgment attest his truth, and the taste relish his beauty? Then, as he enters in, the emotion of reverence or awe rises to bow before him; the affection of love opens her arms to embrace him. Thus the moral action or state of mind which, in the seat of the intellect, carries conviction of truth to the judgment, awakens, in the region of the affections, the feeling of profound veneration; while, again, in so far as it approves itself as beautiful to the taste, it calls forth complacency and love. For, as truth is venerable, so beauty is amiable. What is true is to be revered; what is fair is to be loved.

There is still, however, a third apartment in which these objects of our moral cognizance and observation—these moral actions or states of mind—undergo yet another process. Behind, and farther in than the region of the affections, lies the secret closet of the soul, the seat of self-inspection and self-judgment. From the mind or head, with its twofold faculty of judgment and taste—the discernment of truth and the sense of beauty—through the heart, deeply stirred with the emotion of reverence and the affection of love—there is a passage to the conscience, where the final act in this sifting trial is performed. And here, again, there is a double function, corresponding to the double functions of the other departments. In that sanctuary, that inner court of last resort, these states of mind come to have final sentence passed upon them, and the sentence has respect to the discernment which the judgment has of what is true, and the apprehension which the sensibility has of what is fair. Truth, compelling conviction, and commanding reverence, asks a verdict of acquittal or acceptance, and will have nothing more. Beauty, again, gratifying the taste, and winning the affection of love, solicits a warmer welcome, and would wish to receive approbation and applause. In the one view, there is a demand to be justified; in the other, there is a desire to be praised and to be embraced.

It may be some recommendation of this analysis, or induction, that it combines different theories, and comprehends various principles of our moral nature, which the framers of moral systems have been accustomed to isolate. Thus, the accordance with truth, or the fitness of things, which some have made the foundation of moral judgment (*Clarke, Cudworth*, &c.), and the moral sense or instinct to which others have appealed (*Hutcheson*, &c.), unite and conspire in the first act of simple apprehension, by which the mind takes in the conception of a moral action, or a moral quality, as right and good. Nor is moral rectitude and goodness, on this scheme, a matter of reason exclusively, or a matter of instinct or taste. The emotions and affections have a large share in the work of identifying virtue, and giving it life and warmth (*Sir James Mackintosh*). The emotion of reverence, and the affection or sentiment of love, dealing with what has passed the calm scrutiny of the judgment and the taste, touch the deep springs of holy awe and worship in the soul, and open the fountain of its tears and gladness. Nor does the trial end here. The judge, whose verdict is final, sits within. The moral action, or moral quality, under review, must enter within the vail—into the very shrine, the holiest of all in this living temple—where, on the throne, is the great arbiter, entitled authoritatively to justify what is true (*Butler*), and at the same time, ready, with lively sympathy, to commend what is fair (*Adam Smith*). The award of this ruler of the soul, which is the power or principle of conscience, is conclusive. It determines what is just and righteous, and bestows the meed of commendation on what is excellent and worthy.

But the scheme, as it would seem, has a still higher value. It is in fine accordance with the moral system of the New Testament. For it is no rude or unskilful artist, but a master-hand, that has constructed the noble climax in the Epistle to the Philippians (chap. iv. 8, 9): "Finally, brethren, whatsoever things are true, whatsoever things are honest" (*honesta, σεμνά, venerable*), "whatsoever things are just, whatsoever things are pure" (*ἁγνά, chaste, fair, clean, undefiled, and holy*), "whatsoever things are lovely" (*προσφιλῆ, amiable, loveable*), "whatsoever things are of good report" (*εὔφημα, commendable, such as to move sympathy, approval, applause*); "if there be any virtue" (*ἀρετή, power, stability, firmness*), "if there be any praise" (*ἔπαινος, what solicits and excites commendation*),—"think on these things." There is something more here than a casual enumeration of moral motives. The apostle was too much a master both of ethics and of rhetoric to heap up such materials miscellaneously and at random. There is symmetry in the structure; there is method and system in his fervid appeal. He traces and marks out the double line of approach or entrance, along which actions or qualities, admitted at the door of the mind, are conducted, through the heart, to the conscience. For there are two sets of connected posts of observation in this sketch—two distinct series of successive mental acts. The six names read over in this muster, or roll-call, fall into two ranks; and each of these, at its termination, is represented by a single leader, as in the following tabular view:—

"Whatsoever things are true,"	"Whatsoever things are pure," (*fair*,)
" " "honest," (*venerable*,)	" " "lovely," (*amiable*,)
" " "just,"	" " "of good report,"
"If there be any virtue."	"If there be any praise."

Thus, of these epithets, the first three—what is true, what is venerable, what is just—rank as a column under the one head, virtue; the remaining three on the other hand—what is pure or fair, what is lovely or amiable, what is of good report or commendable—are marshalled in the line of praise.

Or, to change the application of the figure, let us trace the subject of our scrutiny—the particular action or quality, whose moral character is to be ascertained—from post to post, in the citadel of our moral nature. At the gate it is challenged by the faculties of simple apprehension, the judgment and the taste, the sense of natural agreement or fitness, and the sense of beauty; is there in it anything true?—is there in it anything pure? Let it enter. Farther on it has to encounter the emotions or affections, and they have to deal with it—the capacities of reverence and of love must be satisfied; is there anything honest—venerable? is there anything lovely—amiable? Let it pass,—the soul standing in awe of its majesty, and rapt in the love of its gentler grace. But once more it is arrested. One having authority, but at the same time full of sympathy, calls it to account; is there anything just—right, righteous, coming up to the high standard of strict duty? is there anything of good report—worthy, commendable, meet for being warmly honoured and approved? If there be any virtue, any inherent strength of conscious rectitude—if there be any praise, any moral beauty meet to be applauded—then, by all that is true, venerable, and right, in the stern integrity and firm standing of that virtue, and by all that is pure, amiable, and worthy in the fair and soft charms of that praise or that commendableness, and in its warm yearning for sympathy—let us be adjured, let us be persuaded to give earnest heed and full practical effect to that gospel, whose highest aim it is to restore and re-adjust the whole moral nature of man, so that truth and righteousness, grace and love, may once more meet and embrace each other, in the holy home of a reconciled and renovated soul.

Were further illustration needed of this complex system, it might be found in the discrimination, so exquisitely true to nature, which the same apostle makes between two different kinds of character to be observed among men. Magnifying the divine benevolence, as manifested in the death of Christ, he puts it as an all but impossible supposition that "a righteous man" should find a friend prepared to lay down his life for him. He allows it to be more conceivable that "a good man" might win affection thus devoted and self-sacrificing. And he places in strong contrast that love of God, whose miserable objects had neither "righteousness" nor "goodness" to recommend them, but only sin (Romans v. 7, 8).

"A righteous man" is such a one as the poet describes,

"just and firm of purpose," one who is moved by neither fear nor favour from his solid mind. Regulus, calmly turning away from his weeping family and the awe-struck Senate, to redeem his pledge to the Carthaginian enemy, and meet the death prepared for him, with its worse than Indian refinement of cruelty—Hampden defying unjust power—Latimer cheering brother Ridley at the stake—Knox before Queen Mary, and Melville before King James, maintaining allegiance to a Heavenly Master against both the tears and the frowns of royalty—rise as examples before the mind. In each there is a stern integrity—which we apprehend to be "true"—which we feel to be "venerable"—which compels us to recognize it as inexorably and inflexibly "just"—presenting, on the whole, a spectacle of moral courage and steadfast "virtue," almost beyond the reach of our commendation or compassion, such as rather inspires a sort of deep and silent awe. We scarcely presume to praise or pity—we stand apart and reverently look on. But let a touch of tenderness mingle in the scene—let it be the Roman matron presenting to her trembling husband the dagger plucked from her own bosom—"It is not painful, Pætus"—or Lady Jane Grey bidding adieu to her lord, as he passed on to the scaffold, to which she was soon to follow him—or Lady Russell, pen in hand, gazing on the noble features she had loved—or Brown of Priesthill's widow, meeting the rude taunt of the persecutor as he interrupted her in her melancholy task—"What thinkest thou of thy husband now, woman? —I thought ever much of him, and now as much as ever"—or, coming down from the heroic to ordinary life, let it be a character marked rather by gentle manners and kind affections than by strength of nerves, that is exhibited to us ;—and our moral taste is charmed with its "pure" beauty—our heart is warmed with "love" towards it—we speak of it as not only unimpeachably correct, but positively "worthy," and we award to it the meed of our cordial sympathy and "praise." The combination of the two kinds of character, as in some of the instances referred to, is the consummation of moral excellence. To be true, yet, at the same time, not stern or severe, but fair, pure, graceful—to be both venerable and amiable, calling forth in equal measure the emotion of reverence and the affection of love—to stand before the tribunal of conscience and receive, not only the cold verdict which strict justice, caring for nothing more, extorts, *I find no fault*, but that also, which a softer sensibility asks, *Well done*—in short, to be both great and good—such is the idea of a perfect man. Such was He who was not only "holy, harmless, undefiled, and separate from sinners," but also "meek and lowly in heart"—"full both of grace and of truth." Such His Gospel is intended and fitted to make all those who, following, at a humble distance, His example, and changed, by His Spirit, into His image, unite with the "faithfulness unto death" which challenges "the crown of life," "the ornament of a meek and quiet spirit," which not only is of good report and praiseworthy among men, but, "in the sight of God himself, is of great price."

III. Conscience and the Bible thus agreeing, on the

one hand, in the acknowledgment of law, and, on the other hand, in the approbation of virtue, are of necessity closely related to one another. Their mutual relations form the third subject of inquiry, on which a slight indication of the heads or topics must now suffice.

1. In the first place they are to be recognized as distinct from one another, and independent of one another. It may be true, and probably is true, in point of fact, that God never has left us to discover our duty by the dictation of conscience alone, as he has never left us to arrive at the knowledge of his own being and perfections by the discoveries of reason alone. From the beginning God revealed himself and his will, by means of words, to men. He spoke to them of his own character, purposes, and plans. He placed them under an explicit and formal obligation of obedience to an explicit and formal commandment. That, however, does not impeach either the competency of reason to prove the truths of natural religion, or the competency of conscience to establish the principles of natural morality. It is of the utmost consequence, for the interests of revelation itself, to vindicate the independent validity, both of natural theology and of natural ethics; to assert, not the sufficiency indeed, but the legitimacy and trustworthiness, of the light of reason and the jurisdiction of conscience.

2. In the second place, conscience, when once for all satisfied that the Bible is the word of God, bows in lowliest reverence before its paramount authority. She asks, and she has a right to ask, to be satisfied that the Bible is the word of God. She asks this humbly and with

docility—feeling how much she would be the better for the guidance of Him who sees the end from the beginning, who knows all things, and always judges right. She asks it calmly, dispassionately—calling in the help of manly reason to authenticate the voice of the Sovereign Ruler. But being satisfied, she gladly takes her place, beside her sister Faith, at the feet of Him who speaks from heaven; of Him who, coming from heaven, speaks on earth, and speaks as one having authority. She receives the law at his lips. She learns of him what things are true, honest, just; what things are pure, lovely, of good report; what virtue is, and what is praise. And if in any difficult or doubtful instance, there occurs any apparent discrepancy between her conclusions and the clear intimations of his mind, she remembers how an erring understanding, and a wayward will, and her own infirmity or vice, make her judgments at the best but probable,—fallible, even when it is the conduct of man that is judged,—still more fallible when it is the conduct of God. And having confidence in the rectitude, truth, and love of the great Being to whom she owns allegiance,—for to none but a being possessed of these attributes would she, who approves them so warmly herself, yield any homage,—she is content to acquiesce, to adore, and to wait; the rather when she hears such words as these:—What I do, thou knowest not now, but thou shalt know hereafter.

3. In the third place, conscience looks to the Bible for an explanation of much, in the present state of things, that she feels to be anomalous and inconsistent, or at least

incomprehensible. In vain does she look elsewhere for even a tolerable guess upon the subject.

I cast my eye around the world, and long "for a lodge in some vast wilderness." It is not merely that my heart bleeds at the sight of suffering; my bosom swells under the sense of wrong. In the abodes of squalid misery, in the very haunts of reckless crime, what cases innumerable meet my view, not only of injustice at the hand of man, but, it would even seem, of most unequal treatment at the hand of God! That shivering victim of another's lust; yonder little one, bred in filth and profligacy from the cradle; the children of Africa, crushed into brutal apathy or lashed into brutal madness; those sons and daughters of our own happier clime, that, by the force of circumstances, amid the cankering, festering sores of our social state, become well-nigh as degraded as they!—Why are they what they are? What makes them what they are? What chance had they of ever being otherwise? How can these things be, and yet this goodly world be justly governed? Alas! it is little wonder if a sullen fatalism or an angry atheism,—begotten of sad despair, and a vehement resentment of oppression,—reigns among the outcasts, whom neither earth nor Heaven seems to pity! No wonder if, looking on, conscience stands aghast, and feels as if she had no plea to urge in justification of God, nor any word in season to speak to weary man! In vain you tell her of general laws of righteousness and love, which, through inevitable evil, are slowly and painfully working out the highest good. Bid her go with that solution of the mystery into the streets, and see what a scowl of leering contempt or exasperated rage darkens every brow. Let her take it into her own study, and ponder it there: the memory of one beggar-boy, one thin and naked girl, the gaunt face of famished manhood, the sigh of a wasted frame, the sickening groan of a broken heart,—one such dismal vision will scatter speculations by the thousand to the winds. It is darkness all—darkness more than ever. Conscience cannot say it is well, it is good, it is right. But she opens her Bible; she learns there why the race of man is so miserable as it is. Yes. And she learns there also why it is not more miserable still. Sin has entered into the world, and so also has salvation. Sin has entered; it has tainted deeply, it has doomed, the entire human family, and every member of it. Hence these tears, these groans of creation. But salvation has entered too. Hence these tears and groans are not yet, bitter as they are, what otherwise they must have been,—what elsewhere, if not in one only way met and relieved here, they must inevitably be,—"weeping, and wailing, and gnashing of teeth," amid the irremediable anguish of "the worm that dieth not and the fire that is not quenched." Struck and startled; struck with the truth of a representation which, bringing so vividly out the sentence, the respite, the remedy, the issue, really accounts at last for this condemned world's strange and sad state; startled at the thought that, while the respite lasts, the remedy is available for every one, for any one, of its condemned inhabitants;—conscience, the open Bible still in hand, rises in haste from her study, from her knees, and rushes forth on the trembling wings of fear and love, to speak of judgment and of mercy to whatever child of Adam she can reach;—to speak affectionately, for the case is worse than had been thought; to speak wisely, for there is need of delicacy; yet to speak earnestly, for the crisis is urgent; to speak promptly and at once, for the time is short.

4. Once more, in the fourth and last place, conscience finds in the Bible the solution of a problem which vexes her not a little,—the reconciliation of law and liberty. How may virtue or moral goodness possess that element of freedom, of voluntary and spontaneous choice, which would seem to be essential, if it is to be approved as venerable and lovely, and yet retain its original and inherent character of obedience to law? There is difficulty in answering the question; and, apart from the Bible, the difficulty may be pronounced insuperable. The idea of law, and of the supremacy of law, however it may be acknowledged by conscience, is irksome to the will. That masterful power is impatient of subjection to another, and inclined to boast of what it will do if left to itself. If it is to choose the good and reject the evil, it must be of its own accord. To expect that it is to do so upon compulsion and by command, for whatever reward or hire, and yet feel itself to be acting freely, is as unreasonable as it would be to imagine that bribes and blows can give a sense of liberty to the slave, as he drudges doggedly at his master's task. This attitude of the will conscience is at a loss to meet. She owns herself perplexed and at fault. She cannot tame the proud spirit, or win its consent to be under authority.

But she goes to the Bible, and there discovers the charm.

And the charm lies mainly in the insight which she gets into the heart of God, whose holy nature the law expresses, whose just right of sovereignty the law asserts.

That great heart of the Eternal Father is opened up in his Son. God is light; God is love. That law which conscience binds me to acknowledge, the everlasting God acknowledges too. It is the law of his will, and he will himself see to it that it shall become the law of my will also.

Yes; he will himself see to it. For this end, he rights my position, my standing, in his Son, and renovates my nature by his Spirit. The removal of the sentence of condemnation, the passing of an opposite sentence in my favour,—a sentence of acquittal, acceptance, justification,—all in terms of the law, perfectly fulfilled, adequately satisfied; this amazing harmony of law and love in the Father's manner of dealing with me, as represented by his Son, disarms me. My criminal grudge against law, my servile jealousy of law, cannot stand out against treatment like that. My whole soul undergoes a change. The law is in my heart, as it is in the heart of God. It is no more a yoke of bondage to me than it is a yoke of bondage to him. Spontaneously, through his own Spirit moving me,—more and more spontaneously as my heart learns more and more to beat in unison with his heart,—I do the things that are true, honest, just; pure, lovely, of good report; virtuous, praiseworthy. And I do them in obedience to Him whose service is perfect freedom, whose law is the law of liberty.

PAUL PREACHING AT ATHENS:

REASON AND REVELATION.

PAUL PREACHING AT ATHENS—REASON AND REVELATION.

ACTS xvii. 22–31.[1]

"Whom, therefore, ye ignorantly worship, him declare I unto you."

THE discourse delivered at Athens is an admirable specimen of that sound and wise discretion, in the exercise of which, without compromising principle,—nay, rather for the very purpose of asserting and enforcing principle,—the Apostle Paul "became all things to all men." For it was not his doctrine that he accommodated to the views and feelings of his hearers; the truth which he taught was always the same, being the truth as it is in Jesus. It was simply his manner of stating, proving, and illustrating it that he altered, according to the different tempers and different states of knowledge that he found among those with whom he had to deal, that so the truth might have a fair and favourable hearing.

---

[1] "Then Paul stood in the midst of Mars' hill, and said, Ye men of Athens, I perceive that in all things ye are too superstitious. For as I passed by, and beheld your devotions, I found an altar with this inscription, TO THE UNKNOWN GOD. Whom therefore ye ignorantly worship, him declare I unto you. God, that made the world, and all things therein, seeing that he is Lord of heaven and earth, dwelleth not in temples made with hands; neither is worshipped with men's hands, as though he needed any thing, seeing he giveth to all life, and breath, and all things; and hath made of one blood all nations of men for to dwell on all the face of the earth, and hath determined the times before appointed, and the bounds of their habitation: that they should seek the

"He became all things to all men, if by any means he might gain some." This indeed is plainly necessary in every attempt to convince and persuade reasonable beings. We must have some mutually acknowledged principles—some common ground—on which to build our argument; and that ground must be different, in regard to different individuals and classes of men. Thus, in arguing with Jews and with Gentiles respectively, on the truth and reasonableness of the gospel, the Christian teacher had a different course to pursue, according to the different principles, or common ground, which they were severally willing to recognise. With the Jews, he had the common ground of the Old Testament Scriptures. With the Gentiles, again, his common ground lay in what are called the articles of natural religion. Still, the faithful preacher always aimed at the same result,—to bring both Jews and Gentiles to the saving knowledge of God in Christ.

Here, in particular, in the Areopagus of Athens, addressing the chief men of that learned and polite city, the apostle takes a high tone of moral reasoning, well befitting the place and the audience;—the place, that venerable hall of judgment, where, in circumstances not altogether unlike, he who was pronounced by the oracle

---

Lord, if haply they might feel after him, and find him, though he be not far from every one of us: for in him we live, and move, and have our being; as certain also of your own poets have said, For we are also his offspring. Forasmuch then as we are the offspring of God, we ought not to think that the Godhead is like unto gold, or silver, or stone, graven by art and man's device. And the times of this ignorance God winked at; but now commandeth all men everywhere to repent: because he hath appointed a day, in the which he will judge the world in righteousness by that man whom he hath ordained; whereof he hath given assurance unto all men, in that he hath raised him from the dead."

the wisest of men, once pleaded the cause of his sounder faith against the bigotry of his more ignorant countrymen;—the audience, select and choice, claiming kindred with those whose profound and meditative wisdom, on all topics of human thought, is even yet the admiration and delight of the world. Paul meets them on their own field, and partly with their own weapons; yet not sparing sharp reproof, nor shunning to declare the whole counsel of God. For this discourse begins with a bold, uncompromising charge of ignorance regarding what they professed much to study,—the divine nature and the moral state of man;—and it ends with the solemn announcement of an offensive and unwelcome doctrine,—the resurrection of Christ from his vicarious grave. Nay, more, it makes a very pointed and personal application of that doctrine, as proving both the present grace and the future judgment of the Lord. It is thus that the apostle fulfils his purpose, as intimated in these startling words,—"Whom ye ignorantly worship, him declare I unto you."[1]

[1] The following observations of the Dean of Westminster (Dr. Trench) on the English Translation of this verse are interesting and important.—"A great master of language will often implicitly refer in some word which he uses to the same word, or, it may be, to another of the same group or family, which he or some one else has just used before; and where there is evidently intended such an allusion, it should, wherever this is possible, be reproduced in the translation. There are two examples of this in St. Paul's discourse at Athens, both of which have been effaced in our version. Of those who encountered Paul in the market at Athens, some said, 'He seemeth to be *a setter forth* of strange gods' (Acts xvii. 18). They use the word καταγγελεύς; and he, remembering and taking up this word, retorts it upon them: 'Whom, therefore, ye ignorantly worship, Him *set I forth* (καταγγέλλω) unto you,' ver. 23. He has their charge present in his mind, and this is his answer to their charge. It would more plainly appear such to the English reader, if the translators, having used 'setter forth' before, had

The words are startling, and they are full of meaning. For the charge brought against these men of Athens, placed as they were in the very centre and commanding stronghold of the best resources for the highest cultivation of human reason, may be regarded as equivalent to a charge of insufficiency or incompetency against that reason itself in its best estate. And the apostle's bold confidence in undertaking to instruct these learned reasoners, may be held as an assertion of the fitness of revelation to supply the defect, and to help the infirmity of reason. These two points, accordingly, I propose to consider; only premising further, that when I speak, according to the common language used on this subject, of natural religion,—or the religion of reason as distinguished from revelation,—I do not mean to hold, either that natural reason is able to originate such a religion, or that God ever left religion upon earth to be so originated. The first of these opinions is at least very doubtful, and the second is opposed to all history and Scripture; both of which plainly indicate a primeval revelation, imper-

thus returned upon the word, instead of substituting, as they have done, 'declare' for it. The Rheims version, which has 'preacher' and 'preach' after the Vulgate 'annunciator' and 'annuntio,' has been careful to retain and indicate the connection. But the finer and more delicate turns of the divine rhetoric of St. Paul are more seriously affected by another oversight in the same verse. We make him there say, 'As I passed by, and beheld your devotions, I found an altar, with this inscription, To the *Unknown God* (ἀγνώστῳ θεῷ). Whom, therefore, ye *ignorantly* (ἀγνοοῦντες) worship, him declare I unto you.' But if anything is clear, it is that St. Paul in ἀγνοοῦντες intends to take up the preceding ἀγνώστῳ; the chime of the words, and also, probably, the fact of their etymological connection, leading him to this. He has spoken of their altar to an '*Unknown* God,' and he proceeds, 'Whom, therefore, ye worship *unknowing*, him declare I unto you.' '*Ignorantly*' has the further objection that it conveys more of rebuke than St. Paul, who is sparing his hearers to the uttermost, intended."—*Trench on the Authorized Version of the New Testament*, pp. 54, 55.

fectly preserved and gradually corrupted by tradition. All that I mean is to assert, that there is a certain amount of religious truth, which natural reason, having once got the hint, can ascertain and prove,—which, therefore, in whatsoever way suggested, is to be received on the evidence of argument, and which fitly prepares the way for the more proper and peculiar discoveries of revelation, that are to be received on the evidence of testimony, or on the faith of the inspired record of God.

PART FIRST.

The religion, then, of these Athenians may be regarded as representing the religion of natural reason, as it existed in the most favourable circumstances. And that religion is pronounced to be insufficient, not by a jealous and exclusive advocate of revelation, rejecting reason altogether as quite inadmissible in such a question, but by one who himself in this very discourse appeals to reason as good and competent authority so far as it goes, although he holds that it does not go far enough.

"I perceive," says the apostle, "that ye are too superstitious" (ver. 22); too prone, that is, to the abject fear of invisible power. Such is the literal meaning of the word. And such is the essence of superstition. It is to stand in awe and in dread of something formidable,—that something being unseen and unknown. Accordingly, the apostle so explains his own accusation:—"Ye are too superstitious; for as I passed by, I saw an altar dedicated to the unknown God" (ver. 23). Aptly and emphatically taking advantage of this inscription on one of their own altars, he holds them as by their own confession ignorant regarding the object of their worship, and therefore he charges them with being superstitious in worshipping him.

And this ignorance of theirs was twofold. They knew not what God, in his own nature, is; for they believed that he dwelt in temples made with hands, and that the Godhead was like unto gold, or silver, or stone, graven by art and man's device (ver. 24, 29). And, again, they knew not what God is in relation to his creatures,—what dispositions he shows towards them, and how he deals with them; for they conceived of him as likely to be pleased, and capable of being benefited and propitiated, by the offerings of men's hands (ver. 25).

Let these two defects in their religion be considered separately.

As to the first, it consisted in this, that they worshipped God in ignorance of his true nature. They knew him not as a Spirit. They conceived of him as having a bodily structure, and occupying an earthly habitation. They thought that the Godhead might be well represented by graven idols, and fitly and literally lodged in temples made with hands.

Now, in so far as ignorance on this point is concerned, it is not chargeable as a defect on natural religion, or the religion of reason; it is the fault of those who do not use natural reason rightly on the subject. For it is to be observed that the apostle, in refutation of such unworthy and degrading views of God, appeals to natural reason itself as quite sufficient to have taught men better. He argues with his hearers on the principles of their own common sense: "God that made the world and all things therein, seeing that he is Lord of heaven and earth, dwelleth not in temples made with hands" (ver. 24). He who made and who upholds all things, the great First Cause and Ruler of the universe, must be an intelligent mind. He cannot be, as you suppose, like a stock or stone, or any material creature. Your own reason might show that his nature must be a spiritual nature. And, again, this is further evident from the consideration of your own mental and moral frame; as "certain also of your own poets have said, For we are also his offspring. Forasmuch then as we are the offspring of God, we ought not to think that the Godhead is like unto gold, or silver, or stone, graven by art and man's device" (ver. 28, 29). Your own poet has said—We are all his offspring. Now, He whose offspring you are, must possess a similar nature with yourselves. He cannot be a mere idol. There must be a correspondence between the cause and the effect. He who made you rational, intelligent, and spiritual beings, must be a rational, intelligent, and spiritual being himself.

Whether, therefore, we consider the world around us, so full of marks and traces of admirable design, or our own spirits, so fearfully and wonderfully made,—natural reason should suffice to teach us, that there must be a great designing cause, a spiritual Being, whose intelligence pervades all his works. So far human reason, rightly exercised, is a sure and competent teacher of religion, and as such it is elsewhere expressly recognised by this apostle. He declares the apostate heathen to be without excuse on this very account, because "the invisible things of God from the creation of the world, even his eternal power and Godhead, are clearly seen, being understood by the things that are made" (Rom. i. 20). Ignorance therefore, or superstition, on this part of the subject, is not an evil for which natural religion is fairly responsible. Reason, judging from the evidences of design, intention, and contrivance, in the frame of external nature, and in the constitution of our own minds, can confidently announce this fundamental truth of religion, that there is a supreme, intelligent, spiritual Being, whose all-wise energy is above, and around, and in all. "The heavens declare the glory of God." "All his works praise him." And the more we know of the vast extent, as well as of the minute and varied arrangement of these works, the more shall we know of the wondrous, unsearchable depth of the understanding of the Infinite Mind, who planned them all.

It is indeed a glorious and grateful reward of Science —as in her large view she grasps unnumbered worlds, and, following the vast orbs as they roll in unmeasured space, almost seems herself to regulate the majesty of their movements, so that the wandering planet returns after long absence, at the very instant of its appointed time, as if at the bidding of her potent spell; or, again, as with keen and prying eye she searches every nook and recess of this lower earth, and dragging to light the tokens and traces of another world, still finds in them all new proofs of exquisite adaptation, and beautifully adjusted harmony of design; or, again, as she tortures every substance of nature, with more than inquisitorial cruelty, to extort the secret of its birth; or pores with ever-increasing intensity of interest over all the bones, and sinews, and nerves of this marvellous and mysteriously compacted frame of ours;—is it not a glad, and grateful, and glorious reward of Science, in all these her various and wonderful paths, to see, at every step she takes, the almighty hand and the intelligent mind of God? And, instead of impiously arrogating to herself any poor honour for the discoveries which she makes,—what a privilege is hers!—Joyfully and thankfully to ascribe to the Creator alone all the glory, and all the praise, of that consummate, unerring, beneficent wisdom, with which these discoveries show, more and more every day, all his works in all corners of his dominions to be full fraught!

Far, very far be it from any devout mind, out of an unwarranted, unreasonable, and most unnecessary jealousy, to arrest or stay the progress of inquiry, or look with a timid and suspicious eye on any honest efforts made to extend and diffuse the knowledge of nature. The upright search after truth can never be dangerous to him who lovingly engages in it, or dishonourable to Him who is the God of truth. All scope is given to inquiry into all the wonders, whether of the material world without, or of the moral world within. It is your dignity and your duty so to inquire. You are men, and you are commanded to " be men in understanding." As men, you may assert your privilege of investigating all the works of your Creator; and in doing so, you are to follow truth whithersoever it may lead. You are not constituted the judges of consequences and results. Your business is with the facts and principles of truth itself. You are not to determine what should be, or what might be—you are to discover what is. This is the course becoming alike the power and the infirmity of reason. Within this limit you tread surely and safely. Cast aside, then, all alarm as to what may follow from your inquiries. Only prosecute these inquiries with due caution, and put them fairly and faithfully together, so as to ascertain real facts and draw none but legitimate conclusions. And we may fearlessly run the hazard of any inferences which they may suggest, confident that they will all tend to shed new light and lustre on the wisdom in which the Lord hath made all his manifold works.

Doubtless it may be said, and said truly, that such minute and varied investigation of nature is not necessary to evince the intelligence of nature's God. There need not be any such accumulation of the proofs and evidences of a contriving mind, as the great First Cause of all. The argument from design lies on the very surface of creation, so plainly written that he who runs may read. And the statement of the argument, in a single clear instance of indubitable adaptation, whether in the physical or in the mental department of knowledge, is enough to show the existence of a Being not confined to temples made with hands, nor like to any material images, but a Spirit, infinite in power and wisdom. Even the unlearned, from a single such instance, may apprehend the force of such reasoning as the apostle uses, and may see the absurdity of those gross conceptions of Deity which vulgar superstition forms. Still, it is not unsatisfactory to put the question to a more rigorous test, by tracing out more fully and particularly the operations of the divine understanding. And surely every pursuit is profitable as well as delightful, which tends to open up new mines and quarries of natural theology, and to enlarge our views of the Eternal mind,—removing us always to a greater distance from those dumb idols which the heathens ignorantly worship, and declaring to us more and more manifestly the spiritual nature of Him who in wisdom made the world and all things therein; who is Lord of heaven and earth; and of whom we, the intelligent inhabitants ot this earth, are all the offspring.

Thus far, therefore, natural reason is competent to the task of removing, or at least reproving, the ignorance which Paul charges against the Athenians, and giving or establishing right ideas of God as an intelligent being, the source of all design, the father of spirits.

But this is not enough. This does not fully declare to us that God whom we worship. There is a second defect in the religion of these too superstitious Greeks still to be noticed.

To know what God is, as the great First Cause, and the intelligent author of all being, is much. But something more is necessary,—even to know him in his relation to ourselves, or in his designs and dealings with regard to us. This is chiefly important, and is indeed essential to all real religion. This is wanted to complete our knowledge of God, and to impart to our religious worship its distinctness and its depth. All other views of God without this are insufficient.

Thus, if we try to conceive of God and to worship him abstractly, as he is in himself,—apart from all manifestations and expressions of his attributes,—as the eternal Jehovah, the self-existent, who was, and is, and is to come,—dwelling in light that is inaccessible and full of glory,—supremely excellent and blessed in his own infinite perfections;—the mind vainly and painfully labours. Some image of vast and vague sublimity may rise before us, as we strain our exhausted powers in the attempt to hold immensity in our grasp, and to pierce with our glance the gloom of the Eternal. An emotion of awe, astonishment, and stupor may overwhelm us. But no definite idea occupies the understanding; no distinct feeling touches the heart. Our religion is merely a visionary and ideal abstraction.

For relief, we turn the eye away from the direct effulgence of the divine glory, to the reflection of it in the works and operations of the divine hand; and we regard God as the creator of all nature's wonders, and the upholder of all her marvellous economy of the wisest means adapted to the best of ends. Here we tread on solid ground. Here we are in our own proper sphere, and have something substantial that we can seize and retain. And, rising from nature up to nature's God, we can know and intelligently worship the Supreme Mind. Still, such a religion, though not now a dim, doubtful, and sublime abstraction, is essentially defective. It wasn't a definite and pointed personal application. It does not come home to us as moral beings. It does not meet the necessity of our case. It does not satisfy the natural and instinctive longings of our souls.

All men, says an ancient,—all men long for, all men desiderate, or desire, or feel the want of, a God.[1] But what sort of God do they feel the want of? or how do they long to know him? Surely in his relation to themselves. We desire to know, not merely what God is in himself, but what he is to us; or, in other words, what his character is as it may be likely to affect us. This is the question which presses most urgently upon us;—and this question we are bound to entertain. To evade it is to evade what is by far the most important and personally interesting view of religious truth. To rest contented without an adequate and satisfactory settlement of it, is to know God very partially indeed, and so to subject ourselves, if we worship him at all, to the charge of "ignorantly worshipping" him, and of being therefore still "too superstitious."

You do not half know God if it be thus only that you know him,—as the maker of all things, and the father of an intelligent offspring. And yet, alas! there are too many who count it enough so to know him. These are men who profess to be religious, and to be very intellectual in their religion,—far removed from everything

---

[1] Πάντες δὲ Θεῶν χατέους' ἄνθρωποι.—Hom. Od. iii. 48.

like that ignorant superstition which would "change the glory of the incorruptible God into an image made like to corruptible man, and to birds, and beasts, and creeping things." Their Deity is a being of pure intellect,—the spirit or the soul of the universe. And yet, even to such refined worshippers it would not be difficult, according to the apostle's definition, to bring home in another way, and under another form, this very charge of superstition which they so strongly and scornfully disown.

But what! they will say, charge superstition against us—the very folly which we most of all shun? What religion can be more rational than ours? What view of the Godhead more spiritual and sublime? All that in the least savours of corporeal sense, or feeling, or emotion, we carefully and scrupulously exclude—everything like the movements of resentment or desire. The Infinite Mind is regarded as reposing in blessed satisfaction over the wisdom of his works, neither moved, nor at all affected, by anything beyond himself. What is there here of superstition?

So far well. But do you not studiously avoid the consideration of God in his relation to yourselves? Do you take any account of his moral government, his judicial superintendence of your conduct, and his right of authoritative interference in your concerns? And suppose it should turn out, even according to the dictates of sound natural reason, that there is something more to be discovered and known concerning God, than merely that he is the intelligent cause of the order, harmony, and beauty which appear throughout all his universe,—and yet you refuse to consider him in any other light;—who now are "superstitious?" Who now are regarders of invisible unknown power? Of whom may it be said, that in so far as they have any God at all, he is one whom they "ignorantly worship?"

Alas! it is the most melancholy of all delusions, worse a thousand times than all the perverse vagaries of the most whimsical idolatry, to acknowledge a God at all, if you go no further than this. What though it be the truth that you know concerning God, if you seek not to know the whole truth? Are you not still superstitious, —worshipping God ignorantly, and so deceiving yourselves? You still worship an unknown God—known indeed in one view of his being, as the great creative Intelligence—but unknown in what is infinitely more important, his relation to yourselves. To you, therefore, the reproach may still be addressed on the part of those who seek the Lord,—not merely, as you do, in the glorious temple of nature, but, as Scripture teaches and the Spirit enables them, in the temple of supernatural glory also, which is the temple of grace,—"Ye worship ye know not what; we know what we worship."

And what, after all, is your worship? What is your religion? A pleasing sentimental fancy—a poetic figure of personification—a vision of glory and beauty, which lends a living charm and grace to your abstruse researches and laborious speculations. But, alas! it is powerless to reach the heart, and recall it to serious and holy thought. It establishes no fellowship between the Creator and the creature. It calls forth no emotion of reverence, and no sense of duty. It may amuse the mind occupied with the works of God. It will not bring the heart near to God himself. For "he that cometh unto God must believe," not only "that he is," but that "he is the rewarder of all them that diligently seek him."

What, then, can reason do towards settling aright this second and most important branch of our knowledge of God—the knowledge of him as he stands related to us?

Let it be observed how, in reference to this particular, the apostle charges the Athenians with ignorantly worshipping God. They not only worshipped him in ignorance of his real nature; they worshipped him also in ignorance of his relation to themselves. They conceived of him as in some way dependent upon them,—capable of being in some way benefited or pleased by their offerings and services, and likely to be propitiated and appeased by means of them. His friendship, if they desired it, was to be purchased by gifts, or won by flattering obeisance. He was to be "worshipped with men's hands, as though he needed" something from them.

Now mark how Paul treats this superstition of theirs. He plainly and pointedly appeals to their own understanding, and calls upon it to condemn this, as well as the former error. In refutation of such dishonouring views as they had of God's method of dealing with his creatures, the apostle challenges the judgment of natural reason;—"He cannot be thus worshipped, as though he needed anything, seeing he giveth to all life, and breath, and all things." "Thou art my Lord; my goodness extendeth not to thee;"—such is the Psalmist's language;

and it is in accordance with the light of nature and the dictates of man's own heart. All our goodness can never profit God, or acquire for us any merit in his sight. Nor can he treat with us on any such terms as are inconsistent with his own absolute and independent sovereignty.

But what then? What is God's method of dealing with us? Does natural religion tell us? Hitherto it has spoken negatively, to the effect that God is not worshipped with men's hands, as though he needed anything. Has it any positive information on this subject to give? Can it discover to us how he is, as well as how he is not, to be worshipped?

Two things, at all events, the voice of nature tells us, regarding the way in which God deals with men on the earth. In the first place, it tells us of God's impartial bounty to all, as well as of his absolute control over all: "He giveth to all life, and breath, and all things; and hath made of one blood all nations of men for to dwell on the face of the earth, and hath determined the times before appointed, and the bounds of their habitation" (ver. 25, 26). Such is his impartial bounty, and such his providential government, reaching to all circumstances of time and place. But further, in the second place, the voice of nature tells what is the design of that bounty and that government;—"That they should seek the Lord, if haply they might feel after him and find him, though he be not far from every one of us; for in him we live, and move, and have our being, and we are all his offspring" (ver. 27). Such is the view of Providence sanctioned by natural reason. We find ourselves placed under the universal care and kindness of God; and conscience suggests the purpose which that care and kindness are meant to serve,—even to make us seek and find Him who bestows them. We look abroad, and we see the providential bounty of God, and his care of us, reaching to the most minute particular. We look within, and we feel his original design,—and our duty as resulting from that design. Thus far all is clear.

But then, the fact of our sin materially alters the case. For now it stands thus. The providential care and bounty of God are continued and prolonged, while his original design is not fulfilled;—for men do not "seek the Lord, if haply they may feel after him and find him." Hence arises a difficulty as to what God now intends, and how he now appears in relation to us. And this is precisely the knot which reason cannot untie without the help of revelation.

PART SECOND.

It is at this stage of the argument, accordingly, that the apostle calls in the aid of the peculiar discoveries of the gospel; and it is to meet this very difficulty. He states the simple scriptural account of the mystery of God's providence, in regard to men, as consisting in a dispensation of forbearance, subservient to a dispensation of grace, and this again preparatory to a dispensation of judgment.

In the first place, he describes the past dispensation of forbearance;—"The times of this ignorance,"—ignorance regarding his design in placing us on this beautiful and bounteous earth, and watching over us and caring for us while we are here,—"the times of this ignorance God winked at." In the second place, he proclaims the present dispensation of grace;—"But now God commandeth all men everywhere to repent." And in the third place, he announces the coming dispensation of judgment;—"Because he hath appointed a day in the which he will judge the world by that man whom he hath ordained; whereof he hath given assurance unto all men, in that he hath raised him from the dead" (ver. 30, 31).

Thus revelation takes up and completes the scheme which reason in her impotency is compelled to drop.

For reason is perplexed, as well she may be, by the contradictory suggestions of nature and conscience—the wide world without, and the little world of the heart within. Abroad, all nature indicates design,—benignant and benevolent design; we observe not a trace of the reverse, no plan contrived for producing misery. So far as there is manifest contrivance at all, it is wholly for making us happy. The Author of nature is very kind and bountiful. See how he causes the fair face of creation to smile with ineffably attractive loveliness. See how largely, how profusely and prodigally, he showers down upon us the gifts of his bountiful liberality. Is it not he who clothes the common grass with more than a monarch's glory, and provides munificently for the fowls of heaven? Is it not he who made us in mind and body for enjoyment, and who gives us all abundantly the means of that enjoyment? Does not every object that yields us a moment's pleasure attest the good-will of Him who imparts to it the power of pleasing, and to us the capacity of being pleased? Does not every day multiply the proofs of his care over us, and his desire to bless us? Why else does he keep us in safety, and order our lot in wisdom, and cause the lines to fall to us in pleasant places? Why does he load us with benefits, and supply food and raiment, and send joy into our hearts, and appoint kind friends to soothe and sympathize with us, and hope, the bright seraph hope, to animate and cheer us? Surely it cannot be imagined that He who has placed us amid so much that speaks of his own rich and royal bounty, can be otherwise than well disposed towards us. His relation to us must be entirely one of fatherly and friendly indulgence.

And yet, even in the world of nature, full as it is of proofs and instances of much loving-kindness, there are hints of derangement and disorder which might make us pause and suggest a doubt. There are traces and tokens of something wrong,—of something sufficiently alarming,—in the evils which we suffer and the judgments which we bring upon ourselves. There is enough to make us hesitate in interpreting too favourably the indications of benevolence with which all the works and ways of God abound. There may well arise some fear, lest, all-benevolent as the Creator plainly is, his benevolence may be hindered in its exercise towards us by a sterner and severer attribute.

And this fear is strengthened when we turn from the world without to the secret sanctuary of conscience within. There too, a still small voice speaks to us of God;—and of God as possessed of a holy character, and holding a high supremacy;—himself the end as well as the author of creation. Our own hearts, conscious of the dignity and the duty of reasonable beings, tell us of the purpose which, in all his treatment of us, God must be seeking.

And they tell us too of that purpose being unfulfilled. For it is on this very ground—the ground, namely, that all his impartial distribution of this earth's advantages fails to bring us, its inhabitants, to Him as alone entitled to be our Lord, and alone capable of being our chief good;—it is on this ground that our own hearts, conscious of guilt, testify of righteous judgment;—of present condemnation, and of coming wrath. Now, therefore, the question as to what God is in relation to us, becomes more complicated by far; and the mind is involved in painful uncertainty, unwilling to doubt that God is good, yet compelled to believe that in all his goodness he has a holy object in view, and that he is justly displeased because that object is not attained.

It is precisely because "the trumpet thus gives so uncertain a sound," that men so grievously err in preparing themselves to meet their God; and multiply the forms and devices of blind superstition, to appease, as they suppose, the resentment, and purchase the continued bounty of him "whom they ignorantly worship." They feel his care and kindness,—yet they cannot but fear his anger on account of that very bountifulness of his, which they have not suffered to produce its due effect of causing them to "seek the Lord." And in the vain attempt to reconcile and harmonize these opposite views of kindness and of anger, they almost necessarily go wrong.

And you who philosophically pity and despise their error,—what can you do to put them, or to keep them, right? There is indeed a summary method of settling the difficulty which it may suit your convenience to take. You have but to suppress, or modify, or explain away all the evidence on one side, and listen only to what obtrudes itself on the other,—and so to worship God in wilful ignorance of the most important feature of his character. Shut your eyes and your ears to all that seems to indicate any end beyond the enjoyment of God's present bounty, or to threaten judgment for that end unattained; and then you may quietly rest in the flattering belief, that—whatever cause of disapprobation He who made you to dwell on his richly-stored earth may have, because you have not "felt after him and found him"—he will nevertheless continue always, as now, to treat his wayward children with indulgent fondness.

Even you, however, thus partially considering God, are fairly chargeable with superstition; for he is to you in great measure an unknown God. And think not, that the mind really awakened to reflection, or the conscience quickened to a sense of guilt, will be so easily soothed or satisfied. Notwithstanding much experience of care and kindness,—of liberality and love,—the sinner cannot banish the idea of a righteous Sovereign, righteously offended. He receives many blessings, but he trembles lest these very blessings may become a curse. "His own heart condemns him," as not fulfilling the great end of his being; and there is One "greater than his heart," whose condemnation he anxiously labours to escape by all the vain expedients which abject terror can suggest.

"But whom he ignorantly worships, him the gospel declares." It tells the guilty sinner of that plan of salvation which explains all, and reconciles all. It points his view to the cross of Christ,—to the single fact of his atoning death. There, in the cross, love appears,—love infinitely beyond anything that all nature's bounty could ever have taught us so much as to imagine. There too, in the cross, judgment is seen in stern and terrible reality, more than confirming the darkest forebodings of conscience. God is indeed, as nature paints him, nay, far above nature's painting, a God of mercy. God is emphatically, as conscience testifies, a God of justice. Here the conflicting hints which perplexed reason meet and are at one. And now the mystery is unfolded. The enigma is solved. The providence of God is for all practical purposes sufficiently understood, as a providence of present grace and coming judgment. God is not abandoning his claim of sovereignty over us who are his reasonable creatures, dependent on his bounty and subject to his control. He is not unconcerned about our refusal to seek him. He has visited, and he will yet again visit in wrath. That wrath, which Christ our surety once endured, is still impending over us—certain, terrible, inevitable. Meantime, in Christ, God is waiting to be gracious; Christ, our crucified and risen Saviour, averts from us now the doom which we deserve; and grace, free grace, is now proclaimed, and all may freely partake of it. For God beseeches all to be reconciled, and "commandeth all men every where to repent."

But he will not always "wink at ignorance," far less at unbelief. The very cross of Christ, which makes grace free now, makes judgment certain hereafter. Already God has fixed a time; he "has appointed a day in the which he will judge the world," by the very "man" Christ Jesus, "whom he hath ordained" to be a Ruler as well as a Saviour; "whereof he hath given assurance to all, in that he hath raised him from the dead." He hath raised him up for the purpose of grace now; but soon for the purposes of endless wrath.

Two practical inferences may be drawn from the subject and argument of this discourse on Natural Theology, delivered by Paul at Athens.

I. How important is a right knowledge of God above all other knowledge! How necessary is it to take that view of God now which we must take at last. For if we do not, then our noblest pursuits, however pleasing now, will be found in the end to carry their own condemnation and their own punishment along with them, when "that God whom we now ignorantly worship is at last declared unto us."

There is an elevating and ennobling joy in the lofty walks of learning and of science. There is a proud satisfaction in the cultivation of high intellectual powers; nor need it be matter of wonder, if many can give themselves up with intense and untiring zeal to the glorious labour of advancing the great cause of mental cultivation, and enlarging the limits of knowledge. Independently altogether of the triumph of success attained, and the value of discoveries made,—in the very employment of their faculties on themes of such absorbing interest, they experience a sort of calm excitement, a refined and rapturous delight. But, alas! in too many an instance, with all their stores of wisdom, they have not that wisdom which is from above, and with all their gettings they get not understanding. In the almost infinitely diversified tracks which they follow, they scarcely ever meet their God, they scarcely ever fall in with him by the way, nor ever once think of going to seek him, "if haply they might feel after him and find him." Or if, amid the profusely scattered traces of power, wisdom, and goodness, through which they make their exulting progress, they cannot shut out the evidence of divinity,—they may indeed condescend to acknowledge a God; but it is a God with attributes of their own choosing,—a God of their own hearts, not the God of Scripture,—a God of nature, not the God of judgment and of grace. Him they dare not recognise—him they do not like to retain in their thoughts; although in himself "he is not far from every one of them; for in him they live, and move, and have their being;" and although in his gospel he brings very near to them his righteousness and his salvation. But they will not retain him in their knowledge; they put away from them the sense and feeling of his presence. For they cannot but be conscious that on the success with which they contrive to prevent the idea of God from mingling in their researches at all,—or strip that idea of all that might painfully remind them of a yet unsettled personal controversy with him,—much of the happiness peculiar to their favourite lettered occupations must continually depend.

But let us suppose a man of such a stamp to be so placed, that he must exercise his powers and prosecute his discoveries, if he is to do so at all, in the full blaze of all the glory and dreadful majesty of "the just God and the Saviour," intensely revealed to his now fully opened eyes;—let him be left to carry on his once quiet work of inquiry, with a clear and startling apprehension of all the moral attributes of God,—his holiness, his justice, his truth, his love,—all as harmoniously manifested in the Cross of Christ, and all still intolerably offensive to his carnal mind and self-condemned heart;—and where now will be the joy of his lofty enterprise? where the satisfaction of his increasing stores of knowledge? Every object he contemplates is now intimately associated with the idea of a righteous God. Every subject he can examine is full of hints and suggestions of a righteous God. Every new ray of light now reveals to him with more intolerable brightness the righteous God. Every sound carries to his startled ear the name of the righteous God, repeated by a thousand echoes. He can look at nothing,—he can think of nothing which does not speak to him of God, and remind him of duty unfulfilled, and announce the inevitable doom. All his boasted discoveries of nature's manifold works only serve as reminiscences of nature's God, in the character, now terribly revealed, of the God of judgment. And the very capacity which was once his pride and pleasure, the capacity of deep reflection and enlightened inquiry, does but add new stings and tortures to his reprobate mind, by suggesting always, everywhere and in all things, new images and representations of that awful Being, regarding whom he was once ignorant and unbelieving,—but whom now at last he knows,—but knows only as the devils know him,—that, like the devils, he may "believe and tremble."

Compare with this fearful prospect, the sure happiness of him who, no longer ignorantly worshipping God, but knowing him as declared in the gospel, can carry the deep and grateful sense of his reconciliation to that God along with him, in all his researches into the wondrous depths of his creating intelligence and his preserving care. At every new discovery he makes, as not in time only, but throughout eternity, he goes on enlarging his knowledge of the boundless works of God,—he will see ever-increasing lustre shed on the harmony of the divine perfections, which he delights more and more to study. And it will be his blessed privilege to pause evermore in rapture, over the things all fair, and glorious, and good, wherewith the universe is stored, and, lifting an unpresumptuous eye, to say—"My Father made them all."

II. And if the right knowledge of God is thus important, how sacred is our obligation to diffuse it! All sorts of knowledge are interesting, entertaining, useful. This alone is necessary. This will suffice without anything else. Nothing else will do without this.

If Christ you know, enough,—all else unknown,
If Christ unknown, vain though all else you learn.*

Without undervaluing any branch of learning, may we not now assume, according to the teaching of Paul, the utter incompetency of all learning, merely human, to impart and impress those just and solemn views of God's sovereignty and grace, which alone can make men truly wise and good? Men may be taught much out of the book of nature, and yet they may not be taught to know God. Either they will not worship him at all, or they will worship him ignorantly, and, by consequence, superstitiously. It is the word of God—the Bible, the gospel—which alone can fully declare to them that God whom otherwise they must ignorantly worship, as the God of present grace and of coming judgment. By all means, let all sorts of knowledge be diffused. But above all things, let men be taught to worship intelligently a God not unknown; the God who "commanding the light to shine out of darkness, shineth into our hearts, to give the light of the knowledge of the glory of God in the face of Jesus Christ."

---

* Εἰ Χριστὸν δέδαες, κᾂν μὴ γνῷς τἄλλα, σοι ἀρκεί
Εἰ δέ μιν οὐ δέδαες σέο γράμματα λῆρος ἐασι.

THE DUTY OF FREE INQUIRY AND PRIVATE JUDGMENT.

AN ADDRESS TO YOUNG MEN.

THE DUTY OF FREE INQUIRY AND PRIVATE JUDGMENT.

"Prove all things; hold fast that which is good."—1 THESS. v. 21.

THESE two precepts embody two antagonist principles, which, when brought together in juxtaposition, mutually qualify and correct one another; the one, being opposed to that dogged temper which clings to institutions and opinions merely because they are old; the other, to that restless spirit which is enamoured of every proposal of change, for little or no other reason than because it is new. Nor is it simply on the plan of striking a balance, and hitting an average or mean between two extremes, that this combination of opposite maxims proceeds,—according to the doctrine of that ancient school of wisdom, which made virtue to lie in measuring the middle path between pairs of conflicting vices,—or according to the less subtle, but more practical notion of not a few, who would make duty merely negative, and count it the very sum of morality to be free from this error or infirmity on the one side, and the counterpart excess on the other, with scarcely any positive spring of action at all;—as if the swinging of the vessel in mid-stream between the whirlpools, were equivalent to the movement with which it should sweep on towards the desired haven;—or as if the poising of the false prophet's coffin midway between earth and heaven were fitted to be its final rest. Thus to fling together two hostile sins, in expectation of one holy grace resulting from the collision, or the rebound, is but the poor expedient of a lifeless formality, putting the cold and artificial sparks of earth's iron and flint, instead of the glow of heaven's own fire. To say to any one,—Be neither prodigal nor parsimonious; beware of credulity on the one hand, and of scepticism on the other; let not wrath prevail, neither yet be too tame; be not too bold, nor yet too wary;—so to construct elaborately your antithetical see-saw of moral truisms, is to deal with the living soul as if suspense or oscillation between two contrary attractions were its chief good, without either the energy of an onward impulse of motion, or the charm of a satisfying repose.

This is not the moral wisdom of the Bible. It makes use, indeed, often of a kind of antithesis, guarding or explaining a strong and sweeping generalization in one direction, by a counter and corresponding generalization in another. It does so, however, not on the principle of an equilibrium of forces, but rather according to the law of their combination and composition. It gives impulses to the mind, which, instead of neutralizing, conspire with one another; and the result is, not the mere blamelessness of a certain negative prudence, content to avoid extremes and "to dwell in decencies for ever," but the healthy vigour of an earnest and exercised ambition, such as, being temperate in all things, yet striveth for the mastery, and runs the race, laying aside every weight.

In particular, the maxims which this verse unites are not negative, but positive;—"Prove all things; hold fast that which is good." They proceed upon two principles essentially and intensely active,—altogether opposed to mere indolent or passive acquiescence, whether in the authority which would supersede, or in the scepticism which would evade, the exercise of individual responsibility, and the search after what is true and fair.

Thus the precept, "prove all things," casts the soul abroad upon the trial of whatever is presented to us for acceptance;—and enjoins the examination of whatever is thus presented to us for acceptance, on its own proper merits alone; apart from any infallible guidance which might summarily dispose of all questions regarding it. The very thing itself is to be looked at, sifted, and tested by each man on his own account—he is not to take another's word for it. And again, lest this should merely rescue him from the lethargy of uninquiring and irresponsible submission to authority, and hand him over to the apathy of bewildered helplessness,—or that listless feeling of universal uncertainty which the multitude of counsels and of counsellors is apt to cause,—it is intimated that, amid the many things that are to be proved, there is that which will stand the proof—which, in the trial, will show itself to be good—and which, being thus proved to be good, must be held fast. First, "Prove all things;" Then, "Hold fast that which is good."

In illustrating more fully the comprehensive verse under review, we may first consider the general import of the direction which it contains, and the kind of trial which it enjoins; enforcing its practical importance. And we may thus be prepared for considering afterwards the value of the principle involved, in its special application to the season of youth.

I. It is manifestly experimental proof that is here intended,—the kind of proof to which the chemist subjects, in his crucible, the substance which he is examining. It is the testing of metals by fire that is alluded to,—"Prove all things." For it is the same word which is elsewhere used,—sometimes with a direct reference to this process of the trying or refining of metals (1 Pet. i. 7; 1 Cor. iii. 13); and with a covert allusion to it in various other passages, in which it evidently denotes an experimental trial (Rom. xii. 2; Luke xiv. 19; 1 Tim. iii. 10; Gal. vi. 4; 1 John iv. 1).

To such an experimental trial, then, you are to subject "all things." You are to cast them into your moral crucible or alembic, and put them to a searching question in the furnace of your spiritual experience. And you are to deal thus with all things whatsoever that are proposed for your acceptance, whether as remedies of evil or as instruments of good;—you are to prove them all, without exception and without reserve. Nor need you fear to do so, or shrink from the hazard of this proof, lest all the things which you prove should fail, and you should be left to the unrelieved desolation of continual doubting.

There is among them that which will endure; and if, while "proving all things," you are really determined to "hold fast that which is good," the issue of the trial will be assurance and peace.

But, in order to this result, the trial must be earnest, and full, and fair,—earnest as a real, practical experiment, and not a mere idle speculation; full, as not partial and limited, but comprehensive and complete, embracing all the elements of every kind which should enter into the solution of the problem; and fair, as having it truly for its object, not to find occasion for casting all away as vanity and dross, but to seize on what may be prized, and used, and guarded as pure gold. "PROVE," says the apostle, in the first place. Secondly, "PROVE ALL THINGS." And thirdly, Prove all things, that ye may "HOLD FAST THAT WHICH IS GOOD."

In the first place, you are summoned to a sort of *experimentum crucis*,—a process of testing, as it were, by fire. You are to PROVE whatever is presented to you, as metals are tried and proved. In other words, the trial must be earnest. It is as men bent on the settlement of an urgent practical question, that you are to prove all things; as men awakened to feel that you have sins to be forgiven, an eternity to be provided for, and souls to be saved. You are to prove all things, not with the cool indifference and affected impartiality of unconcerned spectators, careless of the result; but with the breathless eagerness of men whose all depends upon the issue.

It might seem indeed, in one view, an advantage to

go to the study of religion and the search after truth with minds and hearts unbiassed and unmoved, with no previous prejudice of education, and no excitement of hope, or anxiety of guilt and fear. Accordingly there are some, even among professedly Christian parents, who have avowed this principle in the training of the young; and there are not a few of the young themselves who, as they advance to manhood, deem it a point of wisdom, or of honour, to qualify themselves for the exercise of a certain philosophic calmness in their spiritual inquiries, by getting rid of whatever impressions of seriousness or of awe the prayers and pious lessons of a holy home have made.

But, not to speak of the impossibility of realizing such a state of absolute equanimity,—even if it could be realized, it would but ill agree with the nature of the inquiry to be set on foot, and the proof to be taken. The things which belong to your peace—which touch the relation in which you stand to the high and holy God, and your eternal prospects of weal or woe—are not to be dealt with as matters of mere abstract speculation; and if you find that you can so deal with them—with the same coolness with which you would cast up a sum in figures, or calculate the movements of a distant planet—so far from being in a fitting mood for apprehending them aright, you show that you are without the capacity of apprehending them at all. The names of God and duty, of holiness and sin, of death, and judgment, and eternity, may be like the symbols or formulæ with which you work an algebraic equation; but of the realities which these names denote you take no account, and form no conception.

Not such is the spirit in which the message of Heaven to dying sinners on earth must be treated by those who would understand its import, and prove all its contents. The very ability to prove all things regarding it implies a previous awakening; and no man will ever truly grapple with this inquiry, until his spirit has been not merely inclined from its even balance, but shaken and deeply moved to its very centre. How vain, therefore, and visionary is the notion of leaving the mind uninfluenced by any suggestions from without, like a sheet of blank paper, equally and impartially open for any or for all opinions to be taken up by it! How entirely contrary is all this to what is implied in proving all things! In fact, this proving of all things in religion never is, in any instance, self-originated; it never is the spontaneous act of the soul simply seeking to adjust its theoretical notions on the speculative merits of conflicting tenets and systems,—at least, that is not what the apostle means when he says, "Prove all things." No; the kind of experimenting which he enjoins is gone into on the spur and impulse of necessity,—with all the interest of a hungry man seeking food—a drowning man catching at a rope —a banished and broken-hearted child longing for reconciliation to his father's bosom.

There is no risk, therefore, arising from the partial dealings and one-sided appeals of parental training and spiritual instruction; nor need you dismiss all your preconceived ideas, from whatever source derived, before you begin to exercise your own judgment on spiritual matters. On the contrary, it is only when the Holy Ghost has thoroughly aroused and awakened you to real personal concern, by means of these very ideas, put into you beforehand, at home, or in the church,—or if not thus, by some other instrumentality of preventing grace,—and it is only in so far as the feelings of intense earnestness, which the Holy Ghost so calls forth, continue to sway and command your whole soul,—that you can either begin, or carry on, to any good purpose, that practical and experimental proving of all things which the apostle here enjoins.

Again, secondly, as the trial must be earnest, so must it be full—complete and comprehensive—taking in all the elements of a right determination. "PROVE ALL THINGS," is the apostle's injunction: put to the question and experimentally test them all. Take nothing upon trust—leave nothing unexamined and unascertained—probe every wound to the bottom—search into the minutest ingredients of every healing balm. See that you are not leaving unexplored some nook or corner in the secret chambers of imagery within; see that you are not overlooking some flaw in the foundation of your house, which seems to stand so sure; make thorough work of your inquiry into all that concerns your relation to the eternal God, and the state of your heart toward him.

Here, especially, there is room for self-deception—for premature confidence and half-unconscious guile. When the spirit of serious inquiry is awakened in any heart, and the disposition to question what has hitherto been assumed or taken for granted,—on a subject of such interest as the saving of the soul,—the anxiety, which can no longer be stifled, must in some way be met and satisfied; and for this purpose the adversary plies all his arts. He would gladly prevent the rising of this prying temper altogether, by the manifold expedients of worldly dissipation or religious formality,—soothing you in your unconcern, and encouraging you to live at ease, as others do. But when he finds that impossible,—when thoughts of unforgiven sin, and an angry God, and a coming eternity, prove too much for him, and the question of your salvation can be staved off no longer,—he must contrive to dispose of it. Nor is he at a loss how to do so. He can shift his ground. But yesterday, he would persuade you that it was fond dotage to trouble yourselves with such matters at all. To-day—now that, in spite of his persuasion, you have troubled yourselves—he must manage you differently. Now, he commends your earnestness: you do well to be interested, and even anxious; you are right in thinking that these things are far too serious and momentous to be left all at sea; they must be proved, tested, ascertained, and settled. And so they shall be; there shall be no blinking of the question now,—no trifling with its awful magnitude; it shall be decidedly grappled with and disposed of. The things about which such uneasy doubts and misgivings have been raised, shall be proved.

And proved they seem to be. For the subtile foe can accommodate his procedure to this change of circumstances, whether in the individual or in the public mind. He would rather, perhaps, that these questions were not raised; but if they are raised,—if men insist on ceasing to be frivolous, and become earnest and serious,—he can deal with that fit or fashion also, and turn it to his own account. He has his plausible solutions of difficulties, when they are started,—his summary and shorthand receipts for cutting inconvenient knots, and patching unseemly and uncomfortable rents in troublesome consciences. If you must look into these things, which perhaps were better let alone, you shall see how they may be arranged and adjusted to your entire satisfaction. You may examine the whole machinery, and try it for yourself. And so the adversary introduces you to a display of skilful legerdemain, and passes upon your unpractised eye many imposing changes and evolutions of specious forms,—as of sacramental mysteries, and church order, and apostolical succession, and fasts, and holidays, and penances, and priestly absolutions,—till at last you begin to think that you have got to the bottom of the whole scheme of salvation. And so, having proved it all, and seen how it is all set in order, you may be contented, and say—Return unto thy rest, O my soul!

Such is the subtlety of Satan, and the fond simplicity of the heart, slow to believe the truth of God, but credulous of all besides. Alas! how ready are men to be imposed upon! Even when indifference gives way to earnestness, as in the days in which we live, and things once treated with entire neglect must be searched, and proved, and settled, how slight a proof will do! How easy is it to raise a cloud of dust, under cover of which the bewildered eye, dazzled by some showy visions in the space between, shall miss the apprehension, both of the bright glory that shines from heaven, and of the pure peace which, under the shining of that glory, may dwell on earth!

But it is not thus that you can comply with the advice ;—Prove all things. On the contrary, the aim of these devices of the adversary is to turn you away from making any personal and experimental trial of these things at all, and, certainly, to prevent you from trying them thoroughly. In truth, the very art of such contrivances lies in the skilful shifting of the question. Instead of the things about which it really concerns you to inquire, and which really need to be proved to the uttermost, other matters are substituted which can be more conveniently and more ostentatiously disposed of. What else can be intended by this thrusting in of the things which concern the Church, and the mystical value of its ordination and its ordinances, when it is the things which concern your own individual peace with your God that have really awakened your anxiety, and which really require to be immediately adjusted?

But prove ye these things for yourselves—prove them all—and prove them thoroughly. Make full proof of your personal reconciliation to God. Be not deceived by any slight healing of the hurt of your soul. Be not diverted from what first and most urgently presses you,—the subject of your peace with God,—by any extraneous considerations, however plausible,—far less allow it to be thus superseded and set aside. Prove all things,—even the things which the adversary would fain impose upon you as a solution or a settlement of the question between you, a sinner, and the holy God. Prove them, test them, practically and experimentally try them, in reference to that very question. Do they really solve or settle it? Do they really provide for the upholding of the sovereignty of the holy law, or the purging of the conscience from dead works to serve the living God? Do they really bring God's controversy with you, and your enmity against God, to an end, and give you enlargement of heart in your walk with God? Or may not this, after all, be better accomplished by the free gift on God's part, and the frank acceptance on yours, of instant and complete forgiveness and favour, on the footing of that perfect righteousness of his beloved Son, which his blessed Spirit enables you to appropriate as your own? "O taste and see that the Lord is good!"

Once more, accordingly, in the third place, the trial must be not merely earnest and full, but also fair. You are to prove all things; not that you may cast all aside as naught, but that you may "HOLD FAST THAT WHICH IS GOOD." If, indeed, the spirit in which you make trial of the things of religion be the spirit of awakened personal concern, and of a thorough-going determination to sift matters to the uttermost, it will be the spirit, not of one impatient of repose, but of one longing for rest and peace. The spirit of impatience, which would unsettle all things, and leave them all unsettled, is desultory and superficial.

But you are in search of a foundation on which you may build; you look for that which, while "proving all things," you may "hold fast as good."

But how, it may be asked, are you to recognize this good? By what test are you to ascertain it? Surely by the test of experience and experiment. For, undoubtedly, the appeal is here made to the self-evidencing power of the truth, and the quality by which that which is really good approves and commends itself to the earnest and honest mind. What that quality is, it may be difficult very precisely to define; for it is a quality to be felt rather than analyzed. But that there should be such a quality is not unreasonable. For, on the one hand, whatever is good is itself of God; and, on the other hand, the trial of it, on the part of the anxious inquirer, is of God also. Both objectively, therefore, and subjectively, God has a hand in this work of apprehending, among the "all things" which are to be proved, the one thing which is to be "held fast as good." Objectively, he ordains the good, and appoints it to be what it is: subjectively, he dwells in you, opening your understanding and renewing your will; and hence a blessed harmony and correspondence between his good and your apprehension of it. And if we observe further, that the distinguishing feature in what is good, according to the ordinance or mind of God, is that it bears the impress of his glory, shining forth in it as its chief end; and that the ruling principle, wrought by God in the heart of him who rightly proves all things that he may hold fast that which is good, is entire submission to his sovereignty, and the full recognition of his glory as being ever of necessity the first and chief consideration to be attended to,—have we not a sufficient explanation of the assurance of faith, grounded on experience? And have we not, at all events, ample warrant for holding that God can verify and attest his own good word to his own people, without the need of any human authority of church or college to countersign it; nay, if he so please, without the intervention of any external testimony whatever?

Surely to teach otherwise,—to allege that one who is moved by God's own Spirit to prove all things, that he may hold fast that which is good, cannot know that good, or be sure of it, on God's mere word alone, unless so-called apostolic men come in with their traditions and mysteries, to set to their seal,—is great presumption, to say the least of it. The ministry and the sacraments are holy and good as instruments; but when they are made to come in between the individual sinner and that God with whom the individual sinner must settle his account alone,—either in or out of Christ, the only Mediator,—they are to be repelled and repudiated, as savouring of the spirit of that man of sin who sitteth in the temple of God, speaking as God, and showing himself that he is God.

Doubtless it is important to have arguments and reasonings of a more palpable nature, by which you may vindicate that which you hold fast as good, and be ready to give an answer to every one that asketh you a reason of the hope that is in you. In this view, outward and historical evidence is valuable. But to your own mind, the best and surest proof is, that you have tasted and seen that God is good. "You have cast your burden on the Lord, and have found that he sustains it,—you have ventured your soul's peace on his word of promise, and it has not failed you,—you know in whom you have believed, and are persuaded that He is able to keep what you have committed to him against that day,—you have heard him yourselves, and know that this is indeed the Christ, the Son of the living God." Yours is neither the shrinking suspicion which, affecting to search all things, will make proof or actual trial of none; nor the supercilious complacency which, with an air of superiority over them all, will condescend to make a selection of what pleases it in each. Yours is neither the vanity of a sceptical, nor the pride of an eclectic, philosophy. You give yourselves to this exercise of proving all things, not as if you were the master of them all, but expecting to find that which will assert the mastery over you,—which will first of all lay hold of you, and which, thereafter, you will do well to hold fast. You go forward in faith,—you go to meet your Lord; and when he makes himself known to you, you are wholly his.

In this spirit you search the Scriptures, and you find that they carry their own authority and their own interpretation along with them. Willing now to do the will of God, you know of the doctrine whether it be of God. Prepared to recognize, as in God himself, so in everything that is of God, the high attribute and prerogative of absolute sovereignty, you see written as with a sunbeam, on every page of the Bible, the uncompromising majesty of his law, and the unfettered freeness of his grace. And convinced of sin on the one hand, and of righteousness on the other, judged also yourselves by the very things which you have been spiritually taught to judge —you find yourselves "apprehended of Christ Jesus." And you cannot but "hold fast that good thing for which he has first of all laid fast hold on you" (Phil. iii. 12).

In this manner the word of Christ is proved by you; and being itself "quick and powerful, sharper than any two-edged sword, piercing even to the dividing asunder of soul and spirit, of joints and marrow, a discerner of the thoughts and intents of the heart,"—that word, as the candle of the Lord, searches your inward parts, and leads you captive to that Saviour of whom it testifies, filling you with "all joy and peace in believing," yea with "all the fulness of God." Blessed experience, surely! Experiment well worth the making! Nor need there be any delicacy or hesitation, any scruple or reserve. God's word can certainly stand the test; and you, fairly testing it, may assure your hearts before God.

So David found, as he repeatedly testifies in his Psalms: "As for God, his way is perfect; the word of the Lord is tried." It is tried or refined,—tested, as silver or fine gold, in the experience of his people. God's word thus stands the experimental test; and accordingly "he is a buckler to all them that trust in him" (2 Sam. xxii. 31; Ps. xviii. 30). "The words of the Lord are pure words; as silver tried in a furnace of earth, purified seven times;"—for "Thou shalt keep thy poor ones, O Lord" (Ps. xii. 6, 7). "Thy word is very pure"—well-tried or refined;—"therefore thy servant loveth it" (Ps. cxix. 140). And

Agur also bears a like testimony: "Every word of God is pure"—it will stand the proof of any trial;—"He is a shield to them that put their trust in him" (Prov. xxx. 5).

So also the Lord himself invites this trial of his words: "Prove me now, and see if I will not open to you the windows of heaven, and pour you out a blessing, that there shall not be room enough to receive it" (Mal. iii. 10). "Open thy mouth wide, and I will fill it." Prove Him—not as the fathers did in the wilderness, when they tempted God in unbelief, asking a sign, and saying, "Can he give us meat in the desert?"—but prove him by proceeding on the faith of his blessed word, and making trial of the grace which it provides. Prove him in all things,—and prove all things in him; and see if "his grace will not be sufficient for you, if his strength will not be made perfect in your weakness."

And the more helpless you are in your destitution and infirmity,—the more utterly at a loss,—so much the more satisfactorily may the experiment be made. Have you sins that are going over your head and sinking you to the lowest hell? Have you a heart that is hard, and stubborn, and rebellious? Are you weary and heavy laden? Are you restless, and dissatisfied, and disquieted with many anxious thoughts and questions which you cannot solve? Ah! go not to any earthly teacher,—build not on any human authority;—prove all things for yourself. It is your own case, and no other than yourself can deal with it—no priest, no confessor, no holy father or reverend brother in the Lord. Call no man master on earth. Devolve on no man the care of your soul. Alone, as if in all the universe of God there were no other poor sinner besides thyself,—nor any saint whose goodness might reach to thee; alone, none of the people or of the priesthood with thee; alone, thou must dispose of this question of thy relation to God, and of all the weighty questions which hang on it. Thy sin is thine own; thy sorrow is thine own; thy responsibility is all thine own. And oh! blessed be God, his word, his grace, his strength, —all, all that is his, is thine own;—thine directly and immediately—thine freely and fully, without any intervention of church or churchman, or sacrament or ceremony —thine through the free Spirit "taking of what is Christ's and showing it to thee;" if only thou wilt consent to "know the things which are freely given to thee of God,"—if only thou wilt "prove all things, and hold fast that which is good." And wherefore shouldst thou refuse?

Such, then, is the kind of trial which the apostle enjoins you to make, in reference to all the things which belong to your peace, or which affect the glory of your God. It must be an earnest, full, and fair inquiry; and an inquiry, above all, directed, not to the unsettling of all things in the spirit of captious scepticism, but to the settlement of the soul in quiet assurance and peace. That he has never deeply believed who has never painfully doubted, is almost a truism, as applicable to the experience of all the higher order of minds. But there are two kinds of doubt,—the scoffing and the sincere. And the distinction between them may be briefly stated. The one class prove all things, that they may find all to be naught; they travel from Dan to Beersheba, and say it is all barren. The other class prove all things, with hearts yearning after something that they may hold fast, and determined to hold fast that which is good.

Such also we hold to be the great Protestant doctrine of the right, or rather the responsibility, of free inquiry and of private judgment; as opposed, on the one hand, to the sceptical philosophy which would deify man's natural understanding, and on the other hand, to the Romish or semi-Romish superstition, which would lay prostrate the individual conscience before the general idol of traditional interpretation and ecclesiastical authority. The true Protestant spirit is not a mere negation, as some pretend, both among its enemies and its professed friends; nor is it to be confounded with the rationalism, liberalism, and latitudinarianism, of modern infidelity. It is not a mere discoverer and destroyer of error;—it is a builder up of truth. It is not a spirit of cold indifference, equally unconcerned about all systems;—it is a spirit of warm and intense zeal; not disposed to doubt, but, on the contrary, heartily eager and anxious to believe. It is the spirit which led Luther through the marvellous experience by which he was fitted for his great work of reformation. He proved all things, —not like the gay apostle of atheistic French philosophy, to catch a flaw in each on which his flippant wit might fasten; he proved all things, if by any means he might find anywhere a place for the sole of his weary foot,—some good worthy to be the object of the yearning spirit of faith that was in him,—the spirit that could have no rest until it attained, not to that sense of universal uncertainty in which the scoffing unbeliever found his miserable satisfaction, but to that full assurance in which, as a meek believer, he might rejoice in peace and friendship with his Father and his God.

It is a poor device of controversy which would confound these two tempers together, and represent them both as equally the legitimate types of the Reformation. But be not ye deceived. Be not lightly defrauded of your birthright, nor, with all its attendant anxieties and responsibilities, be content to sell it for the mess of pottage with which an apostolic Church, or a priestly order, would stay the cravings of your hunger. Rather be content still to hunger and thirst after righteousness that you may be filled;—filled, not with what comes through man's hands, and is cooked up artificially to serve his purposes,—but with the bread of life which comes direct from heaven, even Christ himself, in whom is all the fulness of God,—and with the water of life, which Christ gives, and which is in him who receives it "a well of water springing up into everlasting life." Thus taking nothing upon trust or at second-hand, but hearing for yourselves and judging for yourselves, you will find true and satisfying rest to your souls; and you will go on from strength to strength rejoicing, until at last you appear before God in Zion, where "in his presence is fulness of joy, and at his right hand are pleasures for evermore."

II. The general views which we have been enforcing may

be applied to the season of youth, with special reference to the aspect of the present times.

To explain and enforce the great principle of this text is always seasonable; but it seems peculiarly so in its application to the place which you occupy who are in the prime and vigour of your opening manhood. Considering your position,—engaged as you are in the studies and pursuits of youth, exposed to its temptations, and looking forward to a speedy entrance on the scenes of busy life and of an earnest age,—it is especially important to press upon your earnest regard the precept, "Prove all things; hold fast that which is good."

"Get wisdom," says the wise man; "and with all thy getting, get understanding." In the multitude of your engagements and inquiries, forget not to ascertain the chief good, and delay not to make it your own. "It is good," says the apostle, "that the heart be established with grace;" and it is especially good that your hearts be so established now.

Ah! who can calculate the amount of mischief which has flowed to many a youth in generations now past and gone, from their leaving the question of their relation to God unsettled in their early days, and postponing even the serious raising of it till a more convenient season? How easily do they who so act become a prey to worldly indifference, or religious formality, or spiritual delusion of some sort! Let a young man, who has never learned to bring this question to a fair issue and a final settlement, —who has been familiar with the influences and examples of godliness around him, and has had his impressions, and misgivings, and awakenings, but has never made thorough work of his soul's salvation,—let such a one find himself among sceptics and scoffers,—or even among the gay and the worldly, who care neither to believe nor to deny the gospel;—how is he guarded against the frivolous liberality which, treating with a light jest, or a quaint personal remark, the things which should be thoroughly proved,—the systems and societies, in every one of which there is either God's truth or the devil's lie,—finds good worth holding fast in none of them, or finds it equally in all? Or,—as in these days of increasing earnestness is perhaps more likely,—should he fall into distress and disquietude of soul—should old recollections haunt him, or new relentings come upon him—when he meets with those who have a charm for all his wounds, in the mere name of baptism, or in the routine of church order and the multiplying of church ordinances, what is there to hinder him from laying down his aching head to rest on the bosom of the mother Church that so soothingly invites him to repose in her arms?

How necessary, therefore, is it that you should learn now, ere these trials come, to "prove all things, and to hold fast that which is good!" And be persuaded to make a perfect as well as immediate work of this proof. Begin it in good faith; carry it through with good resolution. Shrink from no pain which it may give, and no sacrifice which it may require. Trifle not with any movements of the good Spirit of God in you; and do not seek a slight or partial healing of the hurt of your soul. Rest satisfied with no plausible presumptions as to your eternal safety,—no vague hopes as to your state, or your heart, being right before God. Search the matter to the bottom. Realize your actual position, as in the sight of Him who is not mocked. Make a thorough surrender of yourself, on the faith of His word who cannot lie. Take nothing for granted, leave nothing unsettled, that at all affects the footing on which you are to be with God, and the dispositions and affections which you are to cherish towards him. Let there be no suspense—no hesitancy here. Why indeed should there be any? How, properly, can there be any? What is the inquiry? Are you at enmity or at peace with God? Are you still guilty and estranged from him, or are you through grace reconciled? Are you on the Lord's side, or on the world's and the Devil's?

Are these not points which can be ascertained? Are they not points which should be ascertained? Was it not for this very end that Jesus died, and rose, and revived, and commanded his gospel to be preached, and sent forth his Holy Spirit,—the seal of your calling and the earnest of your inheritance,—that on these points there might be no more uncertainty, or ambiguous wavering between hope and fear, but full assurance and perfect peace?

O that the young, while yet their minds are keen and their hearts are warm, would consider this—that they would consent to become as little children, and as little children, with full, unhesitating trust, enter, once for all, into the kingdom of God! Be sure it is the vague and unsatisfactory uncertainty in which the question of your personal salvation is left, that exposes you to the danger of being tempted to try Satan's refuges of lies. If only you once make trial of God's own haven of rest,—the heart and home of your reconciled Father in heaven,—no seductions of an evil world, no sophistries of a corrupt religion, will ever prevail with you to seek other relief from sin, or other comfort in sorrow, than God's free grace affords. If only you once realize, in your own experience, the blessed gladness and unutterable joy of that hour when, seeing you afar off, as with trembling steps you venture on the experiment of a return to himself, your Father meets you and takes you into his arms, and with not a word or a look of upbraiding makes you at once and for ever his dear child—never, O never afterwards, would you dream of going back to the husks which you would once fain have eaten!

And if any poor formalist would persuade you that it is the ring on your finger, or the robe on your shoulders, or the shoes on your feet, that constitute your title to your Father's favour, and give you a place in your Father's house—No! you would indignantly exclaim—not these! —all precious as they are, and dearly as I prize them, in their right place, as seals and pledges of my Father's kindness;—not these! If they are to be so spoken of and so applied, I cast them as worthless baubles away. Not these at all are the warrant or ground of my assurance—not any such gifts dispensed, or offices rendered, by my Father's servants—but the free love and sure word of my Father himself, as in the warmth of his embrace I feel the kiss of reconciliation on my lips, and hear his own gracious accents thrilling through all my frame, "This my son was dead, and is alive again; was lost, and is found."

We exhort you to seek assurance before God; to be satisfied with nothing but assurance. We press this upon you, not only as a privilege to be desired, but as a duty to be discharged. It is your only safety amid the divers and strange doctrines with which men are carried about; —it is your only safety amid the manifold devices of Satan;—it is your only defence against mental anarchy on the one hand, and mental bondage on the other;—to have early and thoroughly ascertained for yourselves the truth of God, and your own position before God—to have proved all things, and to be holding fast that which is good.

Be not afraid, in this matter, to go directly to the point—to deal directly with God, and suffer God to deal directly with you. Be sure that "the truth in the inward parts" which God "desireth," and which his own Spirit of truth implants—meeting with the truth which came, with grace, by Jesus Christ, and which the same Spirit of truth manifests to the conscience—this truth within, meeting with that truth from without, from above, and recognizing its majesty and its right to rule, —must insure conviction, so that your soul may "return unto its rest when the Lord hath dealt bountifully with you"—and must give also enlargement of heart, so that you may "run in the way of his precepts, and walk at liberty when you have respect to all his commandments." Pilate, in his helpless embarrassment, may ask, "What is truth?" Priest, or prelate, or holy father, in his fond dotage or lordly pride, may bid you take the truth on trust from him or from his church, and tell you that otherwise you can have no reply to Pilate's question at all. But "if ye continue in Christ's words, then are ye his disciples indeed; and ye shall know the truth, and the truth shall make you free."

CPSIA information can be obtained
at www.ICGtesting.com
Printed in the USA
LVHW101349160422
716387LV00003B/248

9 783752 594638